SHATTERED PEARL

A Taming the Twisted Novella

Jodie Toohey

Wordsy Woman Press

Jodie Toohey
Wordsy Woman Press
Davenport, Iowa, 52806
www.jodietoohey.com

Publisher's Note: This is a work of fiction. Names, characters, places, and incidents are a product of the author's imagination. Locales and public names are sometimes used for atmospheric purposes. Any resemblance to actual people, living or dead, or to businesses, companies, events, institutions, or locales is completely coincidental.

Book Layout © 2014 BookDesignTemplates.com

Shattered Pearl/ Jodie Toohey – 1st ed.
ISBN-13: 978-1-7336236-1-2

ACKNOWLEDGEMENTS

Thank you to Misty Urban for her wonderful developmental consultation and suggestions. Thank you to Kaitlea Toohey for the beautiful cover design. Thank you to Amy Kolner for her attention to detail in final proofreading.

Thank you to all of the curators of historical information both online and off, including, but definitely not limited to, the Clinton (Iowa) Public Library, Camanche (Iowa) Public Library, Camanche (Iowa) Historical Society, Clinton (Iowa) Historical Society, Heritage Canyon (Fulton, Illinois), Muscatine (Iowa) National Pearl Button Museum, Davenport (Iowa) Public Library, and Herbert Hoover Historical Museum (West Branch, Iowa).

Thank you to Midwest Writing Center (mwcqc.org) for all the connections, information, instruction, encouragement, and support.

Thank you to my husband for supporting my dream and allowing me to be the real me. Thank you also to my children, mom, other family, and friends who also may not completely understand me, but who support and love me nonetheless.

Dedicated to
my grandmother, Betty Sinkey, for her love of her little hometown of
Camanche, Iowa, which has inspired my stories.

CHAPTER ONE

Wednesday, June 3, 1908

Pearl. I never knew if the name was given to me as a premonition or a hope, but it was almost inevitable that I'd end up spending my summers on the Mississippi harvesting clams and searching for the elusive gem. I looked out over the river, waiting. The mosquitos swarmed. They sucked the life out of us, drop by drop. We tried to ward them away by rubbing so much sweet grass oil into our pores, that sometimes in the dead of January, we swore we could still smell it seeping out. The bumps itched until we scratched them raw and then they stung. It seemed I could never slather on enough oil; it slid off with the sweat about as fast as I could rub it in.

But the clamming wasn't so bad. We sang as we stirred the cookers of melting mussel flesh. When Lester brought in the next load, I smiled at him, thinking this would be the night. I'd wake up tomorrow, nauseated with child and deliriously happy. I wouldn't have to wait a whole month because I'd know. I was sure of it. I would feel the life growing inside me, working for the day it would burst out, wrinkly, crying, and beautiful.

The babies cried, and I ached. I relieved their mothers' arms at every chance, hoping that motherhood would become a happy disease I could catch. Each time my monthly courses began, I'd feel the blood seep down my legs, and I'd cry. The hope for the only thing that I knew could love me unconditionally, gone.

I thought back as I watched him clamming just offshore as I tossed shells into the cooker. I should've been happy; we were married a few months before on February 17th, when we wondered if winter would ever let go and let spring take hold. And it did, for a day or two, until it suddenly gave way to summer with a crack of lightning and rumble of thunder. I married Lester right there along the river, quickly, to avoid freezing to death. This is where I'd first found him skipping rocks when we were nine, after arriving with my family from Peoria. I'd wandered away after a long-awaited break from unpacking, folding, and placing every item just right to Father's relentless, compulsive liking. Because like Mama said, "None of us are happy until Papa is."

I saw his mass of black hair first from the back, all curly and wild; wet from the river or perspiration, I didn't know. Then I saw his arms, building already with work-worn muscles. He flipped a rock sideways. It skipped five times before sinking, invisible under the muddied water, carried to who-knows-where. I was in awe. The most I'd seen my brother skip was four times. Lester turned, seemingly unnoticing of his grand feat. His eyes sparkled green.

"Hi, there," he said and grinned.

"How did you do that?" I asked.

"Do what?"

"Skip like that, the rock."

"It was nothin'. I do it all the time."

We were fast friends. The barely decipherable jolt I felt as he held my hand to show the angle to throw the rocks grew slowly but regularly until we were 16. And he kissed me. But we still didn't know our destiny. I had wanted to be a wife and mother since I'd received my first ragdoll from Santa at three-years old, but it took a long time before I considered Lester. Then we faced it. We were meant to be together. To share our lives; to become one. After that, there were no arguments; no what ifs. No consideration of parting.

I was determined my children would not grow up tense and guarded as I had. And I knew they wouldn't because Lester was different. He was calm, even-tempered, and, for the most part, flexible. I stoked the fire under the cooker and stood to wait for the flames to catch. I remembered the exact time I decided to make sure my home would be different.

It was the last Friday of April, the 26th, in 1901, early in the clamming season. I was still excited that I'd finally graduated to helping out the adults instead of running around with the children since I was now 13. The sun penetrated the dense east shore's trees early in the morning and got brighter as the hours passed. By mid-day, it was so bright reflecting off the waves in spurts that my eyes began to pain, and I had to look away. The waves slapped together and onto the shore, this way and that. The east wind was cooled by the recently thawed water. Buds popped on smooth river birch limbs with last year's waving green, brown, and brittle. The work was tedious but relaxed. Smelling rotting fish and mud, we boiled the clams until they fell open, and then we pried out the pungent meat and tossed it into barrels to be salted into catfish bait. Though, against hope, we found no lustrous, smooth pearl, we happily chatted and watched the younger children.

Some of them helped us with boiling out. Some of them played. Some of the more industrious made a few pennies toe-digging, wading into shallow water, popping the mussels from where they nestled in the muddy river bottom, and collecting them with their hands. We observed them as we sorted the empty shells by size and shape at the sorting table, a small bed-sized box with three boarded sides to keep the mussels from falling off, saving our backs from having to pick them back up. The shells had different names and were worth different amounts. The not-so-creatively named "pinkys" had a natural pink color so brought more. The ebony shells had a smooth surface with a pearly color and were the same thickness throughout, so made for easy button cutting.

When about a ton of shells had been collected, the men would haul them to Eddie Miller or one of the brothers, Mac, Charlie, or Benny, who weighed them for selling to the button factories, including Holmes and Son on Yazoo Avenue. Even if you never found the elusive pearl, it was like our own little gold rush with payment of $15 to $20 per ton of shells a couple of times each week.

As the sun lowered in that early spring evening, a blanket seemed to descend into my heart. The clam shells, so full of hope just hours before, were hollow shells the local factories couldn't use to be loaded onto the barge that would ply the Mississippi for one of the many button factories down in Muscatine. I looked away from the river and up the shore to see my father approaching, the sun distorting his body to a dark shadow. He tried to be affectionate, patting my sisters and me on the head before shaking my brother's hand, but we were stiff in response, cautious. I breathed a little easier when he kissed my mama and patted her behind; apparently, it had been a good week. My father made more money at the lumber mills in Clinton, so he worked there during the week. Plus, he enjoyed the break from family life. His family didn't mind. My stomach knotted up as I sat down at the dinner table and glanced at the clock on the box which served as a shelf in our tent, 6:17.

My father picked up his fork in one hand and his knife in the other. He slammed them straight down onto the table, making the rest of the dishes jump and a cup clatter to the floor.

"I'm hungry!" he said.

My mother rushed in through the tent's flaps, "I'm so sorry, dear. We had more clams to cook than usual today, so I got supper started a few minutes late."

"A man works all week, he should be able to get a nice, hot meal on time the one night he's home."

"I know. I'm so sorry." She appeared to chisel a wide smile into her face. "It's your favorite."

I could almost see the anger deflate from my father's body as he noticed the mashed potatoes, a cube of butter swimming in a depression in the middle, and a pork chop, the perfect shade of golden brown on his plate.

"Ahh," he said, and dug in. He took a bite of potatoes and spit it out. "There's a lump!"

My mother flew over to inspect the food, poking at it with her fork. "I think there was just the one. Try another bite."

I held my breath and clenched my fists in my lap as my father seemed to suck on the next bite of potatoes, like he was smoothing them against the roof of his tongue like when I eat ice cream. Mama stood and watched, her hands placed one on top of the other, flat on her upper abdomen.

Father winked and said, "Maybe it was something left over from lunch."

Apparently, it had been a good week, indeed, for my father to let such an infraction with his meal go so easily. I, however, felt nauseated from his comment and lost my appetite. I forced myself to eat the food my mother sat in front of me, though, for fear of what would happen should I waste something he'd worked so hard to put on my plate.

Yes, Lester was different. As he was with most everything, Lester's proposal was practical and not a surprise since we'd discussed the prospect on many occasions. Lester said he was ready to start a family, and marriage was the first logical step in the process.

As the clams began to boil in the cooker, I smiled remembering the moment Lester and I got engaged. After church, on May 17, 1908, we walked along the shore downriver away from the clamming camp past the slough. He carried the picnic basket, and I walked slowly to keep perspiration to a minimum. When we got far enough away where we couldn't see anyone else, I spread the blanket out on the sun-toasted grass in the thick shade of an oak tree. Lester set the picnic basket between us and I unpacked it. We ate our biscuits and jam watching the river flow past. We finished and passed the water back and forth until I could no longer stand the frustrated silence.

"Did you get it?" I asked.

Lester grinned. "Get what?"

I rolled my eyes and pushed a loud breath through my lips.

Lester laughed. "Oh, I see. Yes, I got it."

"Well?"

Lester pulled a small silk pouch from his pocket. I waited in anticipation for his words of adoration and sentiment. Dutifully, he pulled himself up on one knee, unwrapped the package, and held the ring toward me.

"I love you," he said, "Will you marry me?"

I waited for more, but nothing came. He extended his arm until the ring, its small diamond perched atop a plain gold band, was inches from my face.

"Pearl. My knee's starting to hurt. Stop teasing."

"Oh," I said. "I love you, too. Yes, I will marry you." I nodded my head for emphasis and held out my left hand. He pushed the ring on to my finger, and I straightened my arm to admire it. "It's beautiful."

Lester swung the picnic basket to his other side, scooted close to me, and draped his arm around my shoulders. We turned our heads to look at each other at the same time, and I could see that his grin matched the one I could feel on my own lips. He kissed me, and soon, our breathing was hard, and we began to lean back. We were at a 45-degree angle when Lester took his arm from where he had been holding me close by my waist and braced himself to the ground with it. He pulled away from me. We giggled nervously and sat up straight. I waited for the feeling to return to my lips.

We didn't need to talk about it. We knew what was expected of us as young folks, and I would've been mortified to have the child we both wanted less than nine months after I was married. Not only had I heard what people said when it happened to other wives, even those late enough where it could've been God's doing, but my father had made it perfectly clear that he would stand for no disgrace being brought upon our family, especially any disgrace caused by that sort of impropriety. Despite the fact my mother talked often about how grandchildren mellowed her father's foul moods, hinting it might do the same for my father, she would be humiliated beyond forgiveness. My face flushed red and I turned away so Lester couldn't see as images of what I dreamed our wedding night would be flashed into my consciousness. I could never have imagined the disaster it would actually become.

CHAPTER TWO

I had looked so forward to becoming Lester's wife. I was ready to give up all my single freedom to be by his side. That's why I couldn't pass up Aunt Gertrude's invitation. Since Lester and I got engaged, not breaching our promise to God became more and more difficult. I found myself glad that I would be leaving to see my aunt in a few days, though I dreaded how much I'd miss Lester because had he not had his wits, I'm afraid I wouldn't have stopped him.

My Aunt Gertrude was no longer a part of the family. My father, if he knew, would've never allowed me to go. Mother and I concocted a story that I was visiting Jane in Chicago. Since her husband's family was well-to-do, he didn't question their ability to pay my fare.

When I worried how my lie would stand up to Father's scrutiny, Mother asked, "When was the last time your father asked you anything and accepted less than 'fine' as the answer?"

I learned early in my life that sickness of the mind was not acceptable, and a memory I had forgotten leaped into my mind. After my Great Uncle Mason, my grandmother's brother, went to the asylum for the last time, my grandmother came to stay with us for a few days, "to help Mother with the children."

One night at dinner, my brother, John Junior, asked, "Where's Uncle Mason?"

Though I was too young to know what was going on, I could still feel the pressure on the room's air intensify, and my chicken caught in my throat. I gulped water to clear it and looked around the table at the grownups, making glances at each other.

Finally, Grandmother spoke up, "He had to go away for a while."

"For work?"

"Well ...," my grandmother said.

"No!" Father interrupted.

Grandma, through gritted teeth, said to her son, "We mustn't lie to the child, John." She was the only person I knew in the world who would dare contradict my father. She turned toward John Junior and smiled. "He went to stay at the Eastern Iowa Asylum just for a little while to rest and get better."

"A hospital?"

"Sort of." My sisters and I all stared at my grandmother, curious about what would next come out of her mouth. Our parents never told us anything; simply dismissed us with, "You go out and play now," or "You'll understand when you're older." The problem was that we never seemed to get old enough, and by the time we did, we forgot to ask the questions again. As I grew up, I realized that's what they were banking on. I kept to myself on almost all matters, never feeling comfortable enough to talk to my siblings about anything of substance, so I never got any answers from them either.

"What then?" My brother would not give up. Usually, this trait in him annoyed me, but this time, I was thankful for his stubbornness.

"John Junior." My father used his end-of-his-rope voice, but I guess with my grandmother there, he felt brave because my brother made no sound to indicate he'd heard my father and sat staring at Grandma.

"John Senior," she said. My father breathed heavy and went back to pulling his chicken off the bone with his teeth, chomping harder than what was necessary to chew the tender meat. "The asylum is a sort of hospital, but it's not for people who have broken bones. It's for people who have other ... troubles." My grandmother sighed loudly, "It's a hospital where they try to fix your brain, dear." She seemed to not be able to find the words and finally just settled on the first thing that came into her head, all at once.

"What's wrong with Great Uncle Mason's brain?" John Junior asked.

"We're not sure. That's why he's there. Don't you worry. They'll be very nice to him, and when he's all better, he'll come back home."

My father shoveled mashed potatoes into his mouth, glaring at his mother. I wondered what Great Uncle Mason would be like "all better."

My father slammed his hand on the table and roared. "Now, that's enough. We won't talk about it another second. Unless or until Mason comes back from his trip, we will not mention this to anyone outside the family. And I don't want to hear any more talk about it in the family either, God forbid anyone should overhear. Your grandmother has indulged you with the information because she is more naïve about trusting children not to talk than I am, but that's the end of it. I will not have anyone in my family be labeled as crazy. Understood?"

All of us, even Grandmother, shook our heads to agree, the children with their eyes wide. Crazy? Grandmother didn't say Great Uncle Mason was crazy, but he must've been, or Father wouldn't have said it. And crazy was something I never wanted to be from that day on. I knew if I was ever crazy, I'd never get to see my family again. I didn't know then that if one day crazy meant getting the truth, it was a risk I would take.

So, yes, my mother and I kept my last solo adventure a secret.

The morning was sunny and clear. It was cool for late July and I hoped my shawl would keep me warm enough. I caught the interurban outside of town, walking out on Chicago Street. Lester had walked me there early so he could get to work on time. I sat on a bench, my legs crossed under my skirt, hands folded in my lap, looking like what I thought must be a sophisticated young woman ready for a grand adventure. The car pulled up, poles on top attached to hanging wires that powered it. I had only seen it a couple of times and had never ridden on one. It was made of sleek, glossy maroon painted metal, rows of arched windows lining each side. I stepped up into the car; it was crowded, so I stood, holding onto a brass pole for the trip to Clinton where I'd board the Twilight Steamboat for Dubuque.

I pulled the letter from Aunt Gertrude from my pocket, unfolded it, and skimmed to the middle of the page to double check my itinerary.

Dearest Pearl,

...Thank you for ... but I have an extended trip to Europe ... I need a change...besides the weather in February ... enclosed a ticket on the Twilight Steamboat to depart Clinton, Iowa, at 10:15 a.m. You should arrive at the Port of Dubuque around 5:30 p.m. My driver will pick you up and bring you to my home. I will have him place a pink rose from my garden into his lapel so you will know who he is. You can let me know how long you can stay and I'll purchase your return fare when you're here, but I propose a week so we can see all of the sights and I can send you home properly spoiled with new pleasures.

My heart started to race as my nerves escalated. I was surprised, based on my tendency for quiet, to have been invited, but my desire for adventure overshadowed my apprehension. A man dressed in black pants and a black collared coat with a brown vest sitting next to me pulled a pocket watch out by the chain inserted into his vest's buttons and flipped it open. I tried to see what was on the clock's face, but he snapped it shut too quickly. He turned toward me and said, "9:43."

My face flushed as I squeaked out, "Thank you."

The river at Clinton was mostly the same as it was in Camanche, flat and sloping gently toward the water, the suspended sand and silt giving it its distinct brown color. Some people's characterization of it as the muddy Mississippi was a misnomer. In the winter with ice on top and nothing to stir it up, the water was clear. I could see fish swimming below and the ice harvested was the clearest and purest I'd ever see.

A walking plank connected the shore to the boat, which was decoratively painted white and baby blue, scrollwork carved into the railings and trim. Porters attached a thick paper tag with my name on it to my larger bag and tucked it away with the other passengers' for safekeeping until we got to Dubuque. I held tight to my other bag holding two apples from the cellar, my brother's handed down copy of Jack London's *White Fang*, a diary, and a pencil. Aunt Gertrude sent me cash to buy food, but I didn't want to spend her money. She told me free lemonade, iced tea, and iced water would be abundantly available.

I sat on the second deck facing Iowa. It wasn't that I wasn't interested in Illinois, but I'd always wondered what Iowa looked like from the river. I'd only ever seen it standing on the shore looking at her close up. I wanted to see what she looked like as the birds and Lester saw her from the clamming boats. I tried to keep my location in mind as we pushed against the current. I'd studied the map my grandmother had tucked safely away in her chest of drawers, but I quickly lost track. It was so green. I didn't know there were so many islands, wild looking with trees growing in every direction, a shanty here or there.

Bellevue was a bustling town with all of its businesses in a row visible from the river, unlike in Camanche. I'd thought it must be Bellevue from the maps I'd studied, but it was confirmed when I overheard the gentleman sitting next me tell his wife. We saw clammers there camped along the shore. They waved and we waved back. The sight of steamboats was common at home, too, and I smiled thinking that now I knew what their passengers see when they wave at us.

I walked around the boat to stretch my legs. The wind whipped and I hugged my shawl tighter around my shoulders. My eyes got heavy so I read my book until I didn't think I could keep them open another second. I wrote in my diary, doing my best to describe the birds, trees, and smoothness of the ride, the lulling waves as the boat created them as it cut through the water. I was careful to make clear letters, but it was much easier than I'd feared. The larger boat made for a much smoother ride than the clamming boats that rocked back and forth.

The clouds increased as we continued north, thickening and darkening, though I only felt one sprinkle on my face. The boat glided into the boat dock; when it was secured with the heavy ropes, they let us disembark. I found my bag and went to find Aunt Gertrude's driver.

I'd never been more than a few miles from Camanche. I knew once I was married and the babies started coming, I would remain within a few miles of Camanche. Though I couldn't wait until I was a wife and mother and knew I would be so happy, I had always felt a tinge of wanderlust, wondering what adventures awaited those who floated by on the steamboats.

I breathed deep and exhaled with nervous excitement; now it was my time for one of those adventures. I was grateful to have this chance and would be happy to have had it when I said, "I do," to Lester.

I saw my name on a small sign the driver held before I saw him. He was short with a large middle and a red face. I lugged my bags and walked toward him. I got within ten feet before he saw me and rushed over.

"Pearl?"

"Yes, sir."

He took my larger bag from my hand. "Are these all your bags?" he asked.

"Yes, sir."

"Please, call me Pete. You travel a lot lighter than your Aunt Gertrude."

"I suppose I need fewer things."

"I suppose so," Pete said, opening the door to the horseless carriage. I'd barely seen any of these contraptions as my father liked to call them, let alone ridden in one. My legs started to shake as I tried to touch the floor but could only find it with my toes. I put my heels down, but almost slid off the smooth seat, so I sat back as far as I could, my legs dangling. I held onto the door handle as Pete maneuvered away from the river and up into the steep bluffs I'd seen from the boat and dock. From there, I couldn't see where the roads went, and I wondered how people reached their houses high up in the bluffs. I soon found out. The roads switched back and forth, snaking their way up the hillside. Finally, it leveled off and we bounced off the road into a half circle lane, stopping in front of the largest house I'd ever seen. I'd seen the house in photographs before when Aunt Gertrude sent her likeness standing on the front porch steps, but the photographs hadn't shown the whole thing, and I'm not sure it would have done it justice if it had.

The house was massive with narrow slats of siding painted blue. I counted seven windows before Aunt Gertrude burst out of her front door and down her porch steps, picking me up in a giant hug.

"Oh, my Pearl. I'm so glad you made it! How do you like Dubuque so far?"

"It's so big. But beautiful."

"How was the trip?"

"Interesting."

"Come in. Let me show you to your room, and then I'll get us something cool to drink."

I turned and saw the magnificent view of downtown Dubuque and the river below. "May we sit out here?" The buildings lined up in rows looked so orderly, and though I knew better, from up there it looked like I could walk to anywhere I wanted to go within minutes. I knew it must be bustling with people, though I couldn't see many of them, and it was quiet. I could see Wisconsin and Illinois though it was hazy from the humidity.

"What a wonderful idea," Aunt Gertrude said, looking out as well. "This is my favorite spot in the whole house."

I knew it would become mine, too. I wondered why Aunt Gertrude would ever want to leave it. I couldn't imagine how Europe could surpass what I saw so far of Dubuque and her home.

*****

The next morning, Aunt Gertrude let me sleep, but someone must have snuck in at some point because I awoke to bright sunlight streaming in through the large east-facing windows. I put on the new dress she had purchased for me for our first day out. It was, I was told, a dress everyone wore in the city, white and decorated with natural colored lace and embroidery. There was also a matching hat. Before putting on the hat, I washed my face, used the water closet, and found Aunt Gertrude sipping coffee on the front porch.

Her face brightened as soon as she saw me. She raised her cup toward me, "How did you sleep, dear? Would you like a cup of coffee? Or I can get Esther to bring you some juice or milk."

I didn't want to trouble anyone, and I'd already resigned myself to drinking coffee as a married woman, so I accepted the brown liquid, adding four sugar cubes. The sun burned my eyes and I turned my head to attempt to lighten its intensity.

"I'm sorry I slept so late. What time is it?" I asked.

"It's not so late. Not even 9:30. I thought after that long trip yesterday that you should get your rest. Besides, we have all day."

I sipped my coffee, burning my upper lip. "I'm sorry I missed Uncle George. I hope he doesn't think I'm terribly rude for going to bed before he came home last night and then sleeping so late this morning. He must think I'm lazy."

Aunt Gertrude laughed. "Don't be silly. He is so focused on his newspaper business, he barely noticed. He will likely be late tonight as well, but he promised me that tomorrow night he would come home early enough to take us to a fancy dinner at the best restaurant in town."

"I don't want to trouble him. I'd even be happy to cook you something."

"Then what would Esther do? She'd be too offended; she doesn't like anyone messing around in her kitchen, even if it's her night off. Besides, you deserve a little wining and dining before settling into married life. So, tell me about this fiancé of yours."

I told her all about Lester, how we'd met, became friends, became more than friends, and how he proposed. She seemed to understand completely when I told her how Lester was such a good worker.

She said, "You'll get lonely at times, but you can never go wrong marrying someone who likes to work. It frees you up to do more of what you want." She leaned over the table and grinned. "Speaking of which, we are free to do whatever we want. I was thinking we could go downtown to do some shopping and have lunch. I also have a little surprise for you."

The surprise was the fourth street elevator that plunged straight down the bluff almost 200 feet over its length of almost 300 feet. It was originally built in 1882 to save the owner time coming home for lunch every day from work. Aunt Gertrude said she liked to take the elevator to avoid all of the automobiles and carriages downtown, plus it reminded her of the tobogganing she used to do when she was a girl, minus the snow and cold. Her face got wistful when she talked about her childhood days. I waited for her to elaborate, but then a cloud seemed to move across her face, and she started talking about all the shops we were going to visit. The ride was smooth; we passed the opposite car on its ascent about halfway down and waved at the passengers.

We shopped downtown, flitting in and out of the bustling stores in Dubuque. The air inside was cool from the shade and fans, providing great relief from the heat and humidity intensified by bodies, horses, and horseless carriages in the streets.

We stopped for lunch and were seated at a table for two by a window with a lace curtain obscuring our view of the people walking by. Or maybe it was meant to obscure their view of us?

A couple the age of my Grandma Hailey sat across from us. They smiled at us and the woman said to me, "Oh dear, you are so pretty. You remind me of my granddaughter. How old are you?"

"Nineteen," I said.

"My granddaughter is 19, also. She's married now with her first child, my first great-grand-baby on the way."

"I'm not married yet, but I am betrothed."

The woman beamed. Her white hair twisted into a bun bouncing as she clapped her hands. "That's wonderful. Congratulations! When will you be married?"

"February."

"That's so nice." The woman grinned and the silence grew uncomfortable.

I didn't know what to say. "You remind me of my grandmother, too."

She shook her head in agreement, a blank look on her face.

"Have a nice lunch," I said, turning my attention to Aunt Gertrude. She rolled her eyes and I laughed.

She shifted her focus to the blurry figures on the other side of the curtained window. "So how is YOUR grandmother, anyway?"

There was a tinge of ice in her words, especially how she emphasized, "your grandmother," failing to acknowledge that my grandmother was her mother.

"She's doing quite well," I said. "She had a little bit of an illness last spring, but she's as spry as ever."

"Still touting the tragedy and praises of her brother?"

"Great Uncle Mason?" Aunt Gertrude didn't respond. "She doesn't talk about him a lot."

Aunt Gertrude's face looked hard, like she was clenching her jaw. I wanted so strongly to ask her about her relationship with my father's family, and what they did to drive her, and more importantly, did to her to *keep* her away, but I didn't know what to say. I opened my mouth to ask the question, but the words stuck in my throat and I was left with my mouth hanging open. Then the moment passed. The waiter brought our food, Aunt Gertrude's face softened, and she started to tell me about all of the wonderful restaurants in Dubuque that she intended me to experience.

After lunch, we walked up and down the streets going in and out of more shops. Aunt Gertrude found a dress, so I sat in a plush chair to rest my feet while she went to try it on.

I was looking around at all of the fine ladies shopping in the store when I heard the scratch of a curtain being opened and Aung Gertrude's startling voice, "What are you doing to that little girl?"

I swung my head to see a man helping a little girl of about four button up a dress, her flat, bare chest exposed.

The man sprung up. "What are you doing?"

"I ... I needed to try on this dress," she said, holding it, draped over her arm, toward him. "I didn't know it was occupied. Clerk! Clerk!"

The man's face reddened as the little girl hugged his legs and he patted the top of her head behind his back.

As the clerk approached, Aunt Gertrude yelled across the store, "This man was undressing this little girl right here behind this curtain."

The clerk looked at the man, confused.

"Yes, I was," he said. "This is my daughter." Tears started trailing down his cheeks. "My wife …" He sucked in his breath and swallowed. "My wife just passed away and my daughter needed a new dress." He continued through clenched teeth, "She is too young to dress herself and I don't know what size she wears, so I was helping her to try it on."

Starch seemed to evaporate from Aunt Gertrude as her shoulders slumped and she dropped the dress she was planning to try on. "Oh, I'm so sorry," she said. "I didn't know. I'm so sorry."

"Now, if you'll excuse us." The man yanked the curtain closed.

Aunt Gertrude grabbed my arm and pulled me to stand. I didn't know what to do. I'd have liked to have comforted her and said that it was just an innocent misunderstanding, but I couldn't find the logical connection between what she saw and what she apparently thought was happening. On the way out, Aunt Gertrude whispered to the clerk and then we stopped at the checkout counter. Aunt Gertrude lay cash I assumed was enough to pay for the little girl's dress.

I tried to enjoy the rest of the day. Aunt Gertrude and I were both quiet. I didn't know what she was thinking about but I couldn't stop wondering what happened to Aunt Gertrude to make her react that way.

CHAPTER THREE

The months after my trip to Dubuque and leading to the day I wed Lester passed in a blur. Then, just like that, our wedding day, Saturday, February 15, 1908, had come and closed, and it was the next day. The light through the windows had brightened, telling me dawn would soon be rising. I'd rolled over with dampness on my cheek, my pillow still wet from the night's tears. The morning was not what I'd thought it would be when I woke up after my wedding day. And now I'd have to walk into church, hoping everyone wouldn't be able to read on my face the way I'd shamed my new husband.

I looked over at Lester, his bare work-sculpted chest rising and falling in perfect rhythm. I'd imagined this morning for months, picturing turning to face Lester, a content smile of satisfaction on my lips, feeling confident our child was already growing inside. It was the opposite of reality. I tried to swallow the sob forming in my throat.

The ceremony was beautiful but brief; when it ended at 5 p.m., our guests went to the reception. We stole another kiss as husband and wife at the back of the church before joining them for cake and coffee. My stomach itched inside, and I could tell that Lester, as I did, wished we didn't have to attend the reception. We were able to leave around nine, feigning exhaustion.

At first, it was everything I'd imagined it would be. Tender kisses. Anticipation. And the promise of creating a life with the person I loved and adored more than anyone else. When the time came, I thought I was ready. But feeling like someone had taken a clam knife to my insides, I screamed out.

Lester jumped back. "Are you all right? What happened?"

"I'm sorry."

"Do you want to stop?"

I shook my head no and closed my eyes.

Perched above me, he kissed my forehead and moved toward my lips until the passion in me built. When he tried again to complete our consummation, I tensed. I took deep breaths and concentrated on relaxing, but it was no use. A terror I'd never felt before seemed to take hold and closed me as tight as any locked door. Lester rolled away, propped his head on his bent arm, and looked at me, worried.

Tears started to slip from the outside of my eyes, into my hair, and onto my pillow. "I'm sorry. I don't know what's wrong."

Lester pulled me toward him and wrapped his arms over my naked breasts, clasping my upper arms. He kissed my hair. "Shhh. It's all right. Don't worry. We don't have to do this tonight. We can try again later."

"But I want to," I said. "We talked for so long about how we wanted a baby as soon as possible."

"I know, but a day or two won't make much difference." He gently pulled my face toward his and stroked my damp hair. "Don't worry. It will be all right. It's been a long day. Why don't we just get some sleep?"

I nodded in agreement.

He whispered in my ear, "I love you."

I choked, "I love you, too," and let my tears slip out, suppressing my sobs. It was only a few minutes before I heard Lester's breath settle into sleep. I rolled out of his embrace to the other side of the bed, afraid he'd awaken, but he didn't. What happened? What went wrong? Why was I so afraid?

We were good, waiting until our wedding night to give in to what sometimes felt like overwhelming temptation. So I knew it wasn't Lester. But what was it?

The night grew darker and then brighter as the moon rose. I don't remember when my tears finally relented to sleep.

Lester woke up and lifted his head, providing a shadow from the now bright sun so I could squint and see.

He smiled. "Good morning, wife."

I smiled, too, but immediately remembered that last night wasn't a dream. "Good morning," I mumbled and got out of bed. "What time is it?"

"7:43."

I rushed to the kitchen, calling over my shoulder, "I'll get coffee and breakfast on right away." At least those wifely duties, I knew I could accomplish. I stoked up the wood in the stove, ground coffee beans, and scooped them into the pot. I pulled the new cream and sugar set my aunt Sally had given us yesterday as a wedding gift out of the box waiting on the table. Lester had installed a pump that deposited water into a sink, a luxury I was grateful for, especially in winter. I lifted the handle up and down, filled the set with the cold water, swished my fingers around their insides, and rubbed my palms over the delicate purple flowers painted on the porcelain surface. I laid the creamer pitcher upside down on a towel. I grabbed the sugar bowl. It slipped and I held my breath as it clanged into the sink. I closed my eyes and picked it up. A small chip was missing from one of the handles. Though I tried to hold them in, I couldn't. The tears flowed.

Lester came up behind me. "What is it? Let me see."

I held the damaged gift up to him and he took it.

"It's only a small chip. Don't worry." He searched the sink, reached in, and holding a piece of porcelain in front of my nose, said, "Look it's barely a sliver. I'll stick it back on and nobody will notice."

He rinsed the sugar bowl and set it down, right side up, next to the creamer pitcher and pulled me toward him. I turned it over before sinking into his arms.

"Everything will be all right," he said. "You'll see."

I composed myself and managed to brew the coffee. Lester filled the creamer pitcher with the cream staying cool in the icebox; and he filled the cracked bowl with white sugar cubes. My hands shook as I used the tongs to splash two into my coffee and pour in the cream. We sipped our coffee in silence. "Breakfast." I jumped up.

"Let me do that. Besides, I'm not all that hungry and it's almost time to get ready for church."

I pictured all of those knowing eyes on us, speculating on whether I was already carrying Lester's child. They would snicker as they all did after a newly married couple walked into church. "I don't feel up to church. Do you think we could miss it this one day?"

Lester grinned. "I think the Lord will forgive us this once. After all, we could still do the Lord's work." He winked at me. "I'll get the eggs. Then we can make breakfast." He cleared his throat. "And go back to bed?"

I nodded yes. Maybe last night was a fluke. Perhaps it would go easier today. I pulled a pan from the cupboard and placed it on top of the stove. Then I pulled bacon wrapped in parchment from the icebox, noticing that it would need to be refilled with more ice soon. I might've felt guilty that Lester was doing what most women would consider my duty, but I could tell he was getting restless and wanted something to do. Before he was anything else, Lester was a hard worker, always needing to be doing something productive. He often got restless on Sundays, especially in the winter when there was nothing else to do.

At least when it was warm, we could go for walks. Early in our marriage, I would resent Lester always choosing to work over spending time with me, but eventually, I would learn to accept it. And even appreciate it when there was something around the house that needed done.

Lester set the bowl of eggs down and stood next to me. I looked over at him and let a nervous laugh escape my lips. "What are you doing?" I asked.

"When you're done there, I'll cook the eggs."

I shook my head. "No, I'll do it." I playfully pushed him away with my flat palm against his chest. "You're a married man now. You're supposed to be sipping your coffee while I do the cooking."

"But I want to help."

"You can help by staying out of my way." I smiled as I remembered the countless times I heard my grandmother say that to my grandfather. I pushed away the thought that my mother never had to say anything like that to my father.

When the bacon was crisp, I pushed it to the pan's side and cracked eggs over the bubbling fat, slowly to prevent the whites from flowing too thin. I tapped two yolks with the edge of the broken shell so they would spread and cook through as I liked them. I stopped my arm in mid-air before doing the same to Lester's.

I called over my shoulder, "How do you like your eggs?"

I heard a shuffle approach from behind.

"What was that?" Lester asked.

"How do you like your eggs? Hard or runny yolks?"

Lester squinted his right eye and paused. "My ma always flipped them over, but I guess they were still soft. How do you like your eggs?"

"Hard yolks; flip them over and keep cooking them until they're done. And when you think they're done, keep them on a little bit longer."

"Huh. I didn't know there was any other way to make eggs."

I laughed. "Me either, until I went to Jane's house and her mama made them without flipping them over. Not only were the yolks runny, but the whites were still clear, too. But I had to be polite, so I gagged them down. All day, they roiled in my stomach." I looked at Lester to find him grinning. "I just knew I'd vomit that day, but I never did. My father insisted that his yolks be pale as a yellow-tinted ghost and mama never made a mistake. I'd have hated to have seen it if she had."

Lester kissed me on the side of my head above my ear. "Well, I will love them however you cook them." As he walked away, he said, "For truth; I won't pretend."

"I'll try to flip them like you say, but I can't guarantee they won't break in the process."

We ate our breakfast in silence, an excited tension between us. I was anxious to try again but still nervous. So I lingered at the dishes, taking extra care to ensure they were clean with not a speck of soap residue. When I finally turned to him, Lester sipped his coffee, watching me, his eyes shining.

I cleaned my teeth and joined Lester in our bed. We lay facing the window with nothing between us, like the new spoons his Aunt Abigail had mailed us from South Dakota, with her regrets she couldn't chance traveling for the wedding in the volatile Midwest February weather.

I felt him grow against me and heard his breath quicken. Mine soon matched and I turned to face him. He kissed me lightly at first, hesitant, but I slipped my fingers around the back of his head and pulled him toward me. I relaxed onto my back. His hand traveled down my body; I relished in it until it passed my navel. I tensed. I tried to shake this feeling of fear gripping my middle away as he rolled on top of me, parting my legs. I thought of the baby I would eventually hold in my arms as I opened myself to Lester, but just as he was about to complete our union, I slammed shut. He tried to get through, but I was impassable.

"I'm sorry!" I pushed myself up from beneath him to a sitting position. I shook my head and crossed my arms tight against my chest.

"What is it? Did I hurt you?"

"Yes. But it's not your fault. I don't know what's wrong. I just tense up." I pulled the sheet around me as I bolted out of bed, frustrated and confused. I hugged it tight and stared out the window.

"Are you thinking about something?"

"No," I lied, choking. "No. I want to," I said, turning to him. "Please believe me. I do."

He stood and I saw his persistent readiness briefly before he pulled his knickers from where they were draped over the headboard and put them on.

"I know," he said as he finished dressing. "It'll be alright. It might just take more time. I need to use the outhouse."

I dressed, obsessing over why in heaven my Great Uncle Mason's face jumped into my head as Lester's touch reached my lower abdomen.

CHAPTER FOUR

It was our one-week anniversary and we'd yet to truly become husband and wife. For my parents, Saturday night was the night, and I expected it was the same for all married couples. I hung the curtain, removed the wash tub from the hook, and started preparing the bath.

"I'm getting the bath ready," I said. "Do you want to go first?" In my family, father started the bath and we worked our way down to the youngest, who jumped in and back out due to the water getting cold. My father, when he was in a good mood, kidded, "Don't throw out the baby with the bathwater," which got plenty of groans as we got older.

"No." Lester laughed. "It makes more sense for you to go first. After I use it, it'll be so filthy you won't want to get in." He held his hand out to me; the dirt was thick from doing his chores, in some spots it looked like he was wearing a sweater. "Just don't get too much of that perfumery stuff in there. I don't want to smell like a funeral when I go to church tomorrow."

"I won't."

A warm, leisurely bath would've been so welcome, but even though I'd left Lester staring contentedly at the fire in the fireplace, I didn't want to leave him a cold bath. I washed and dabbed on rose water after I got out. I combed out my hair and let it fall wet down my back. It dripped though I'd tried to get all the water out with a towel. I put on my nightgown and robe, pulled the curtain back, and saw Lester slumped in the chair, asleep, a glass with a couple of swallows of brown liquid held loosely in his hand resting on the chair's arm.

I cleared my throat. "I'm done," I said. Lester's eyes opened slowly. "What're you doing?" I asked.

"Every Saturday night, my parents would share a bit of whiskey. I thought it was a good idea. Would you like some?"

Maybe it would help. "Sure."

"Take this, if you don't mind sharing my glass. There's just a swig or two left. I'll get my bath and then we'll have a little more together."

I took the glass from him and took his place in front of the fireplace. I'd tasted whiskey before. Father certainly had plenty of it available. I didn't like it, but I so wanted to share something with Lester that I hoped the taste would improve with my maturity. I smelled the liquid. It had a slightly smoky and sweet odor. I held the glass to my lips and tipped it until I felt it touch. It burned. I opened my mouth to take in a sip, swallowing it as fast as possible. It burned its way down to my stomach. And then I began to feel warm, so I took another sip. By the time I finished what was left with the third sip, it was tasting quite good.

Lester and I had a wonderful night. After his bath, I sat on his lap as we watched the fire dwindle and sipped another ounce or two of whiskey. I was relaxed and thought I was ready. But as soon as we went to bed and tried, I closed up again, vague thoughts of Mason touching me shutting me down.

*****

I sat up in bed, watching the full moon's light dance across Lester's bare chest as the unusually warm nearly mid-March wind blew through the curtains. The fabric scratching across the window's wood frame got to me, so I jumped out of bed, tied them away where the breeze couldn't catch them. I leaned against the sill; it felt good on my back through my thin, white nightgown. I watched Lester's face, so peaceful. His face smooth from his nightly shave and his chest rising and falling in gentle waves. I wanted to be close to him and thought about getting back into bed to rest my head on his chest. But I'd disappointed him enough already. I knew I couldn't finish what I'd start. I took my diary and sat in a chair next to the window as far away from Lester as I could get while still getting enough moonlight to see what I was writing, as if somehow words could solve my problems.

The pencil poised on the paper, but nothing came out. After all, what could words do? They were just light grey marks in patterns. They meant nothing to anyone who didn't understand the patterns and assign meaning to them. The paper blurred as tears filled my eyes. I snapped the journal shut, my pencil wedged into the spine. I heard a crack as the cover bent.

I thought back again to my great uncle, Mason, pouring over every moment I spent with him around in my mind, trying to figure out why thoughts of him came into my mind whenever I tried to lay with Lester.

I remembered one night when we'd all went to visit my grandmother when Great Uncle Mason lived with her. It was supposed to be a fun, family reunion. We took a couple of our smaller camping tents so we could sleep in the yard. It was one time my parents actually seemed happy. We set up our tents and laid out our blankets on the ground. The clouds were darkening and I hoped it wouldn't rain.

My sisters and I slept in one tent with me closest to the flap that served as a door. I woke up in the night to feet shuffling outside. I peeked out to see Mason wandering back and forth through the tents. My heart pounded in my throat. I worked out my plan in my mind.

He's old and frail. If he tries to come in here, I'll scream, kick him, and push him back out. I'm stronger than him now. I can fight him off.

But why would I need to fight him off? Other than boiling in me a feeling of terror I couldn't explain, I couldn't remember anything else he'd ever done to me. I just had this inexplicable fear that told me to stay away from him and keep my sisters away from him, too. I watched. Whenever they got close to him, I couldn't take my eyes away.

On the rare occasion when he'd talk to them, I'd interrupt and take them away to play or do some made up chore.

Maybe I should just tell Lester. But what would he think of me? I already felt like I didn't deserve him enough. Felt lazy whenever he came in from working to see me reading a book or writing in my diary.

I never thought much about my great uncle, Mason, before. I never thought it peculiar that he lived with my father's mother; he was just always there. When I was older and realized this wasn't a typical living arrangement, I'd asked my mother about it. We were snapping the ends off green beans, getting them ready for canning. She said when my great-grandparents died, Mason lived with his sister, my father's mother; the other siblings wouldn't have him. My curiosity overshadowed my usual bashfulness.

I asked why.

My mother sighed and looked uncomfortable. "I'm not sure I should tell you," she said. I looked at her, widening my eyes. "I suppose now I must, though," she said. I agreed with a nod. "I'm sure you've heard about the war between the states?"

"Yes."

"Great Uncle Mason, Papa's uncle, fought in the war for the Union Army. He came back ... well, broken."

"Broken?"

"He wasn't the same person as he was before he joined. He was sullen, angry, and easily startled. I was always on edge when we lived with your grandparents and he wasn't locked away in his room." I looked at my mother sideways. "Yes, even more on edge than now. Anything could put him into a fit, but mostly it was loud noises, like if someone dropped a dish. He'd scream this high-pitched wail and hide behind the furniture. Your grandmother had a way of whispering to him to calm him down and get him to go to his room and lie down again. When anyone would try to talk to him, it seemed like he wasn't there.

His eyes would appear like he was far away in his own head somewhere."

I remembered that. And I remembered feeling the uneasy fear
whenever he was around; I didn't know what, but something told me to
stay away from him. I listened as much as I could.

"And then there were the rumors and Aunt Gertrude ran away."

"Aunt Gertrude? What does she have to do with it?"

My mother looked even more nervous, her voice wavering, her
hands shaking, and her face reddening. "Oh, nothing. They said it
wasn't true."

"What wasn't true?"

She pretended she hadn't heard me, set her bowl of beans down,
and walked into the house. I knew then I had to drop the subject. But I
kept wondering about Aunt Gertrude and Mason and if it had anything
to do with the scene she'd made in Dubuque.

CHAPTER FIVE

The nights we tried always ended the same. I'd wanted to consummate, but I involuntarily and unrelentingly tensed up as Lester began to enter me. After that, he stopped approaching me; I think he was waiting for me to initiate. But I couldn't. I was too afraid of what might happen. And the thoughts of Great Uncle Mason kept invading, though I tried to push them away.

Other than the lack of what's required to produce a child and being close the only way a husband or wife can, Lester's and my marriage was almost everything I'd hoped; the only complaint I had was not getting to spend enough time with him. We woke together each morning, just as the sun created a sliver of pink on the horizon, peeking through the lines of naked trees. As winter relented to spring, we followed the sun, getting up earlier and earlier, the trees sprouting and blocking more and more of its promise. I fixed him breakfast and concentrated on household chores while Lester worked at the cutting factory creating button blanks from the shells harvested the previous season. He returned for noon dinner long enough to gobble up what I'd prepared, and then he'd go back out. After completing the day's chores, we had supper and settled in for the evening. Sometimes he'd bring the *Clinton Herald*; he'd share the contents and we'd talk about them, often quipping jokes along the way. Sometimes I read aloud from the latest book I was reading. And at other times, we'd just sit in comfortable silence with me doing needlework and he smoking his pipe, staring into the roaring fireplace. Often, he was buried in his ledgers, plotting and planning. Increasingly, though, I wrote in the evenings about what I'd seen out my window, what I remembered, and I tried to get at the memories eating me away.

Whenever Lester and I had tried to create life, he hesitated, waiting for me to signal him to proceed. But I couldn't. Then one night, more than just a vague memory of Great Uncle Mason suddenly appeared. I could feel the color drain from my face. I rushed away from Lester and to the outhouse. As I sat there in the dark, it flooded in. I was sitting on my great uncle's lap under a blanket. He was rubbing my belly, but his hand slid down too low over my thin nightgown. A panic flushed through me and I jumped up and away. I looked to my father and grandmother to see if they'd noticed; they were still deep in conversation. I looked at my great uncle, but somehow, he didn't seem to be there; his eyes were somewhere far away.

I was brought to the present by Lester knocking on the door.

"Are you alright?" he asked.

"Yes. I'm fine. I just had to go really bad." I winced, knowing a lady did not discuss her bathroom habits with anyone. I relaxed slightly as I heard Lester walk away.

Then another memory appeared. It was during an overnight trip my father, my siblings, and I took to my grandmother's when he'd decided my mother wasn't measuring up to the standards set by his own mother. Thankfully, there were only a few of these trips, and when I was old enough, I refused to go because of the fear. My great uncle had lived with his sister since returning from one of his stays at the Eastern Iowa Insane Asylum. He had lived with my great-grandparents after the war between the states, but they'd passed away by the time he'd been released. It was only a few weeks after the previous incident, and though I'd already heeded my internal warning to stay away from him, I didn't know why. I woke up from where I slept on the floor in the sitting room to find him perched on the chair, staring toward me with his eyes far away, his manhood dangling between his legs. It was the first time I'd seen an adult penis and only the second time I'd seen any. The first time was my brother's when I'd accidentally walked in on him getting out of the bath; after quite a scolding, he remembered to latch the door thereafter. Horribly, and even though I only saw it a moment, I'll never forget that first view of the adult male genitalia: wrinkled and drooping, like a worn-out shoe dangling off a stick. I clamped my eyes shut, rolled over, covered my head, and pretended to be asleep, my heart racing. Within a few seconds, he'd gotten up and shuffled away. I peeked out from under the blanket, making sure he didn't come back.

Once these memories came to me, they wouldn't leave. They haunted me, filling me with a despairing wondering if there was more locked away. I also began thinking again about Aunt Gertrude and the little girl in the dressing room. Did we have something in common besides our want to travel? Why didn't these memories come to me then? I knew I'd never be able to bring myself to ask her.

Thankfully, the start of clamming season arrived and there was no time for dwelling on troubling thoughts, so I did my best to shut my memories away. On April 20, 1908, we arrived on the Mississippi River shore and set up camp by mid-morning. It was a windy, clear day. A dead log lodged in the shallows, imprisoned by mud. There were small, muddy pools where the river had flooded over but was unable to return to the channel. The surface was a mottled green and brown as the sediment suspended in the water mixed with the reflection of the blue, cloudless sky. Sometimes the waves would get ahead of themselves and topple over like a child who had not yet learned how to run, its top moving faster than its bottom. White foam rolled over and dissipated to bubbles until it was gone.

The men started clamming while we women prepared the cookers. They tested their methods just offshore and we watched. As they inched the boat forward, they dropped the net adorned with clawfoot clam hooks into the water. As this drug over the river bottom, the clams viewed it as a threat and clamped on so the men could simply pull them out of the water into the boat. There were two of these, one on each side of the Jon boat, so the clams could be removed from one while the other was used to harvest more clams. Lester said sometimes they got in such a smooth rhythm that it was almost like they were dancing. To help control the boat, a three-foot by four-foot piece of canvas in a frame with iron weights at the bottom, called a mule, was attached to the boat to help navigate the strong Mississippi currents. Some days, the men drifted miles downriver, so they had to row the boat full of clams back up.

We finished setting up camp. After the stakes were pounded in the ground and the canvas secured over them, we put everything away, organized and convenient. We waited for the first batch to arrive for cooking out. I felt safe there despite the thick cover that could've hidden anything wanting to betray my trust. Since the moment Lester and I were married, I was rarely alone, but lonely. The ruminating lured me like the drink to some of the men I'd known growing up. And I had to fight daily to try to keep the thoughts away. I was drowning in the thoughts and fears, *What happened to me, and why?*

Even though I knew it was coming, when the blood seeped down my legs, I cried. The hope of a new life vanished each month, leaving a pocket of empty despair.

CHAPTER SIX

After clamming steadily for almost two months, I was glad to get a break to see my best friend, Jane, visiting home from Chicago. Though her parents were relatively well-to-do compared to my family and most of the rest of Camanche, one wouldn't know it unless she took them to her house. Jane dressed plainly in a shirtwaist and brown skirt, like the rest of us.

I met Jane years ago at the clamming camp. She walked by one day and asked what we were doing. When I explained we were clamming, she was fascinated and came back ever since to help. Jane met her husband at the Camanche Club when he was visiting from Chicago with his family. When they were married, Jane moved to Chicago to be with him. She wrote to me that she was home visiting her parents and invited me for an afternoon of catching up over lemonade. I thought maybe I'd tell her about my marriage troubles with Lester, but I was so ashamed, I didn't know if I could get up the nerve.

We sat on the edge of the bed in Jane's old room. She must've sensed my dilemma. She asked, "Is everything alright? You seem quiet, even more than usual."

"I'm fine," I said. "Just a little tired."

Jane giggled. "A lot of late nights, I suppose." She sipped her lemonade and then sighed. "I remember those early days. Aren't they wonderful?"

I could feel my cheeks blush as I concentrated on trying to focus on anything else out the window.

"Oh, come on, Pearl," Jane said. "It's me. We're adults now, married women."

I shrugged. "I guess I'm just embarrassed."

"Then that is even more intriguing. But I won't pressure you. If you ever want to talk, I'm here." She put her crystal glass to her lips as I thought I heard her say, "Maybe I could learn something."

We talked for several more minutes. I told her about the latest clamming and stories of pearl discoveries I'd heard. She told me all about Chicago. Eventually, it seemed like we ran out of things to say and were comfortably silent for a few minutes.

"You must say, 'Hello,' to Mother," Jane said as I drained my last swallow of lemonade, the not-quite-dissolved white sugar coating my tongue. "She'll never forgive me if I let you leave without doing it," she said.

Jane's parents had taken to me right away. They'd often said how grateful they were that Jane found such a grounded family to spend time with and learn from. They had built up their wealth from humble beginnings and often fretted over how they would teach Jane the value of hard work and enterprise. Their worries died away when Jane met the clamming families and took a liking to the activity.

The sitting room was dark with the shades pulled. Jane's mother sat in a rocking chair, engrossed in a book.

Jane knocked on the wood door frame. "Mother."

Jane's mother didn't stir.

"Mother," Jane said louder. Mrs. Hardenbacher looked up. "Mother, Pearl's here."

Mrs. Hardenbacher grabbed a piece of ribbon from where it rested on the arm of her chair, stuffed it into the book, slammed it shut, and set it on the table next to her. She clapped her hands. "Pearl, my dear. It's so good to see you. Come in." Jane's mother pulled the heavy curtains further apart, letting in more natural light. "Let me get some light in here so I can get a good look at you. My eyes can't stand the sunlight when I'm reading, and it seems the only way I can read for any length of time without getting a headache is to read by this lamp." She pointed to a Tiffany piece on the table; its stained-glass shade created colored shapes on the floor where the sun streamed through. "Sit down and tell me all about how you've been getting on."

"She can't stay long, Mother. She's got to get back to camp, and Father and Jesse will be home soon, so we have to get supper going."

"Yes, of course, dear. A woman's work is ongoing isn't it?" The room became awkwardly quiet. I couldn't stand the silence and had to break it. I tried to think of something, and my eyes landed on Mrs. Hardenbacher's book.

"What were you reading, Mrs. Hardenbacher? It looks like it's interesting."

"It's called *Ten Days in a Madhouse*, written by Nellie Bly. Have you heard of it?"

"No. What's it about?"

"It's rather old now," she said, flipping pages. "1887 the copyright says, so over 20 years ago. For a newspaper story, she got herself committed to the Blackwell Island Asylum in New York and wrote about all the awful things that happened there."

"How did she get in there?"

"She pretended to need a place to stay. Some ladies took her in, then she talked about worrying everyone was crazy, wouldn't sleep, and moped. So they decided she was insane and got her committed."

My imagination arose with a tension in my shoulders. Asylums would have records. If Great Uncle Mason had confessed doing something horrible to his niece or great-niece, it would be in the records. If I could see the records, I would know the truth. If I could know the truth, I could get beyond it and lock it away forever. *Maybe I can get into the asylum, too,* I thought. "It sounds interesting. I would love to read it," I said.

"I only have a couple of chapters left. I'd be happy to loan it to you."

"That would be wonderful. How should we arrange to get it to me?"

"Let me see," she said, examining the number of pages between the ribbon and the book's end. "I have chores and such to do, so by my calculations, I should be able to get the rest of it read within two or three days. You could stop by any time after that to pick it up."

"I don't want to rush you. Will that be enough time?"

"I'll make it enough time. It'll give me a good excuse. I'll tell Jane's father, I'm sorry but I just must finish this book so I can pass it on to Pearl Sinkey," she said, winking. "Speaking of Sinkey, how are the newlyweds? Is Lester turning out to be the fine husband everyone thought he would be?"

"Oh, yes, he's wonderful." Anticipating the next question that inevitably comes, I said, "And he'll be home soon wanting his supper, so I'd better go and get mine started, too."

I escaped without being forced to tell the shameful lie that the timing had not been right yet to become in the family way, which was much more bearable than the truth that after almost four months, Lester and I weren't even truly, 100% married.

The 72 hours following passed more slowly than almost any I'd known before. As soon as the clamming boats untethered and slipped away from the shore, I told Mother I had an important errand to run and would be back in plenty of time to boil out the first load. I ran all the way to Jane's childhood home. Luckily, Mrs. Hardenbacher was sitting in a rocker on her front porch, the book in her lap. She stood as I ran up the steps, out of breath and wet with sweat. Somehow, I just knew that book would be the ticket to figuring out how to get the information I needed.

"Perfect timing," she said. "I just finished. You won't be disappointed." She handed me the book.

"Thank you. I can't wait to read it, though I'm not sure how long it will take. When did you need it back?"

"Keep it as long as you like. Jane isn't interested in literature nowadays. We have so many books already that if you never bring it back, we won't even notice."

"I'll bring it back," I said.

"Can't you stay a while?" Her eyes opened hopefully, and had it not been my certainty the conversation would've turned to children, the favorite topic it seemed for long-married ladies when talking with the newly betrothed, I would've liked to spend some time leisurely rocking on a porch in the fresh air. But fortunately, or unfortunately, I had already proved myself a liar for being gone longer than I'd said.

"I wish I could, but I must get back. If anyone finds a pearl, I want it to be me."

"As it should be, given your name. It's almost your birthright, isn't it?"

"I'd say so." I laughed and waved back, Ms. Bly's book practically burning a hole in my pocket the words were so hot to get into my head. Whenever I had a spare minute, I read. I held the book in one hand while stirring clams with the other. In the evenings, I read instead of writing in my diary. Lester had given up on loving me weeks ago. He brought me a candle in a pink flowered holder one day as a gift and said when I was ready, to light the candle as a way to tell him without embarrassment. The wick stood straight and white and the dust accumulated to be wiped away during my weekly cleanings.

I pondered my options. It had been more than 20 years since Nellie Bly wrote her book. Surely conditions in the asylums had changed, if not because of her book then with the passage of time. I was afraid. Every night, I thought about lighting Lester's thoughtful beacon, but I couldn't. I felt him drifting further and further away from me as he became quieter and quieter in the evenings, no longer telling me all about his day. I had to do something. Though I'd hoped asylum conditions had changed, I counted on the way to get in to be the same. I started to plot my plan in my head.

CHAPTER SEVEN

It was unusually cloudy and cool for mid-July, and I was growing tired of what I assumed were wondering looks about how I had still not announced I was in the family way, an assumption based on how everyone's gazes seemed to drift straight to my abdomen. Aunt Gertrude had written that she had decided to make her European trip permanent. I thought fondly of my excursion to see her a year ago and wished I would've thought, and been brave enough, to ask her more about her separation from the family. And now, when it mattered more, it was too late. I couldn't go to Europe, and it hardly seemed proper to ask her such a thing as if Mason ever did anything improper to her in a letter. So I had to stick with my plan.

We got word that Grandma Hailey was feeling ill, so I volunteered to ride to Low Moor where she lived with my Aunt Elsie and Uncle Arnold to check on her. As much as I kept to myself with others, with Grandmother Hailey, I seemed to open up. She was so much easier to talk to. Though what I really hoped was that my grandmother was able to tell more about Mason and his stay at the asylum, which all I'd heard about were through hushed whispers when they thought I wasn't listening.

Aunt Elsie hung clothes on the line. When she saw me, she threw the wet garments into a basket and ran up to me.

"Pearl. It's so nice to see you. Is everything alright?"

I slid off my horse and tied it to the hitching post, which having been driven into a large boulder, had me in wonder for years as to how it got there. "Everyone is fine from my place. We got the word that grandmother was ill, so I was sent out to check on her and pay a visit."

"How sweet!"

A cool drop on my hand made me look up to the sky. A dark cloud was approaching quickly.

"Oh, dear," Aunt Elsie said, "Would you help me get these clothes down before I have to start over? I was afraid the sky was look-ing like rain, but it was so nice and cool, I had to do something to get me outdoors."

We pulled the clothes from the lines and piled them into the basket, getting just inside the door as the rain came down in white sheets splattering the mud.

Aunt Elsie laughed. "We made it." She set about hanging the clothes around the house while I went upstairs to see Grandma Hailey.

Her door was open an inch, and the white painted wood, the ridges of past coats pushing through, was rough on my palms as I gently pushed the door open. Her hair was a mix of bright white and dull grey, hanging loose over her shoulders. She leaned against several pillows in a semi-sitting position, her eyes closed, and her mouth slightly open.

"Grandma," I whispered.

Her eyes fluttered, blinked, and finally settled on my face in recognition.

"Pearl! You've come," she said.

"Yes. We'd heard at camp that you weren't feeling well."

Grandma slapped her hand through the air. "Awwww. I'm fine. Just a few aches and pains is all. Sometimes my mind forgets my body isn't as young as it used to be."

I pulled the rocking chair, getting goose pimples as it scraped against the floor, and set it as close to the bed as I could. "Are you feeling better?"

She winked. "If I say, 'No,' will you stay a while?"

I laughed. "I will stay a while either way. Father sent a message to Mama that she was to visit in his place as soon as the clamming could spare her, but I offered to come instead."

"A welcome substitution," she said.

"For which?"

"Both!" Her eyes crinkled with a broad smile, and she patted my hand. "Now, tell me, how is the clamming going? Any pearls for my Pearl?"

I shook my head and gave her all of the statistics I could remember. I sensed that Grandma was tiring, so I resolved to take my chance on broaching the topic which was my secret purpose in coming. I waited for a quiet moment. "Grandma, I've been wondering about Great Uncle Mason."

Grandma scooted herself to a more upright position. "Oh," she said, "you have? Such a dear boy he was."

"What happened to him? I know he fought for the Union in the war between the states and that he died at the asylum, but that's all, and other than him being at your house, I don't remember much about him." *Except for feeling a dreadful terror whenever he was near*, I thought but didn't say.

"He was such a good boy. Always carefree and running around, full of energy. He was a sweet boy, too, very thoughtful. Never failed to remember my birthday and pick me some flowers. He said when he turned 18, if it was still going on, he was going to join the Union Army and 'teach those rebs a thing or two.' Mother, of course, was dead against it and tried everything she could think of to talk him out of it. But as carefree and thoughtful as he was, he was also stubborn. And Father was proud that he was willing to do his manly duty. So he went." She stopped and rubbed her throat.

"Are you thirsty?" I poured water from the pitcher into the metal cup on the stand by her bed. "Try this."

She took a sip. "Thank you kindly, Pearly, that was just what I needed. Now, where was I?"

"You said Great Uncle Mason joined the Union Army."

"Oh yes. He went and we heard regular from him for a while, and then nothing. Mother was so worried that something had happened, and she'd never see him again, but we reassured her that his name had not shown up in the casualty rolls, so he had to be alright. Everyone was so joyous when the war was finally over. Though it didn't take long for it to turn to sorrow when Mr. Lincoln was killed. Two weeks later, Father and the other men were just bringing in the next load of clams when here comes Mason down to the shore." Grandma chuckled. "Mother got so excited, she dropped the ropes and boy did everyone scramble to the Jon boat before it drifted back out into the river. We followed her as soon as we could, but our great relief at his return right quick turned. He looked so old, dirty, and disheveled. He just stared straight ahead as we hugged him and Mother helped him get washed up and into fresh clothes. Where's my hankie?" She reached into her nightgown pocket and dabbed the corners of her eyes with the neatly folded cloth.

My selfish interests were suddenly overcome with mature concern. "Do you want to rest now, Grandma? I can come back later or another day?"

"No, no, dear. It actually does me good to remember. Don't mind my tears; seems with age you lose the will to fight them back. Mother tried everything she could to bring our sweet Mason back. She read to him, cooked his favorite foods, and told him the news of all he missed while he was away. Father told her Mason would be okay, just to leave him alone. He said it takes a while for a man to get used to not being in a war. Mason was mostly silent, a grunt here or there, but absolutely no conversation. And, of course, we were all anxious to hear about the war. When one of us would drop a cup or plate doing dishes, he'd jump up into a fighting stance and put his arms up. The most he ever said was one night when we woke up to the shrillest screaming you ever heard. We went in to find Mason curled up under the bed, screaming like someone was stabbing him."

"Did he hurt anyone?"

"No, but Mother was afraid he would, so that's when he went to the asylum. After a few weeks, they declared him cured and sent him home. Apparently one day, some young schoolmates were scuffling in the street playing war, and they tried to get Mason to join in. But Mason ended up folded like a baby in the middle of the street. They took him back to the asylum. He stayed nine months that time. While he was there, both our parents died so he came to live with me and your grandfather when he got out. After that, he was quite a bit better for a while. He worked and talked, though still nothing about the war, and he had no more such dramatic episodes, but he was still quiet a lot, startled at loud noises, and seemed to go in a trance, like those spiritualist mediums, but without bringing word from the dead."

I tried to calculate the timeline in my head, figuring out where the time we lived with my grandparents fit into everything. Grandmother answered for me.

"As he got to his late thirties, just before the time you, the folks, and other children came to stay, he went downhill. Your grandfather just couldn't take it and sent him back to the asylum before giving him a chance to have a screaming fit or curl up in the street. They had to put him in a straight-jacket, because he screamed and tried to run away, saying they wanted to kill him." Grandma wrapped her arms around her chest as if she felt a sudden chill. "He never came back. He died there. He knew he would. He wrote to me about how they were slowly killing him. He said he'd behaved shamefully, but he didn't say what. I assumed he'd killed someone, but it was war, and I wrote back that if it was that, it was nothing shameful, and if it was something else, I'd forgive him. But he never got a chance to explain."

I thought about asking about how Aunt Gertrude fit into all of this, but when I opened my mouth, no words came out. I just couldn't think of a way to ask that wouldn't embarrass myself or upset her. On the Hailey side of my family, it was as if Aunt Gertrude was even more dead than Great Uncle Mason because no one uttered her name in Hailey company.

Grandma closed her eyes and leaned back. Her breathing became deeper and more regular as she drifted off to sleep. I watched her, wondering if Mason's confession of shameful behavior had anything to do with my own recollections. Was there more? Something worse? Something so terrible my mind wouldn't even allow me to remember? I had to find out.

CHAPTER EIGHT

I remembered the articles I'd read about the treatment of mental illness. Lobotomies and electroshock that left patients shells of themselves. And straight jackets; as I thought I wouldn't be able to stand being that restricted as anxious I got when enclosed in small spaces. This fear stemmed from my childhood when one of my brothers, as a prank, blocked the privy door so I couldn't get out. He forgot about me, and I wasn't found for almost an hour when my mother had to go. My brother was in deep trouble, but my mother did not dare tell my father for fear of the beating he would give. But my brother's guilt ran deep anyway and he treated me extra special for at least two weeks. I suppose until he figured he'd repented enough and provided enough amends.

I had to get more information, to see if Grandmother thought the asylum was as bad as in Ms. Bly's book before I tried to go there, so on Thursday, August 13th, I told Mother I'd promised to go to Grandma Hailey's and work on needlepoint. She would never argue because Father would not have anyone break a promise to his mother.

My grandmother and I sat side by side, engrossed in our own projects. Mine a sampler to hang on the wall for Lester and I and hers a mixed collection of unidentifiable figures. My proud grandmother wouldn't admit her eyesight was too poor for needlework, or perhaps she thought I wouldn't visit if we didn't have our projects in common. So she sewed randomly, and when it was time to change thread, she'd pretend it was a bargain: me threading her needle while she got me a cookie or something to drink. I looked out of the corner of my eye to see that she had plenty of thread on her needle so no reason to avoid what I was about to ask.

"Was Uncle Mason happy to go to the asylum?" I asked, though I already knew the answer.

"The first time he was indifferent, but the next time, he put up quite the resistance. Which was more of an indication of how much he needed to be there."

"Why's that?"

"The asylum was a lovely place. I was almost jealous I couldn't go. It seemed like it would be a holiday."

"What did it look like?"

"The building was large, almost like a castle, made of stone, with large windows. The lawns were sprawling and green with lots of paths to walk and flowers to admire. It had the most beautiful roses on bushes all in a row along the perimeter. They let us visit with Mason in one of the sitting rooms. It had to be as comfortable as any of the richest parlors in the big cities. I just wished I could sit in one of those plush chairs all day and read."

"But Great Uncle Mason didn't like it?"

"He was so out of his mind, dear, that he wouldn't have liked anything. The friendly attendants – they always asked how we were doing and were smiling at the residents – explained that part of the illness was not being able to recognize and appreciate comfortable surroundings. I simply didn't see how he could complain. They served us some of the food. It was delicious. Meat, potatoes, fresh rolls."

"What sort of treatment did they give to him?" I asked.

Grandmother jerked up, her eyes confused. I was afraid too much silence had passed. "At the asylum," I explained.

Her eyes clarified to the present. "Nothing much, really. Just rest, relaxation, and talking. The wonderful doctors assured me that was all Mason needed. Not those terrible treatments the very severe had to endure. They spoke with Mason every day to try to get him to open up and come to terms with what he'd faced in war, and the fears that still plagued him. He insisted he was fine. But thankfully he didn't ever get really violent." I watched my grandmother's eyes become more glistening. "I often wonder if those other treatments may have helped Mason. He insisted he was fine. Just had nightmares, but the doctors kept saying he was insane. Then it was too late."

I reached over and lay my hand over my grandmother's. It felt soft and loose, like a wrinkled, newborn kitten's skin. "I'm sure they did all they could, Grandmother." She nodded her head slightly and put her other hand on top of mine.

I hated to see my grandmother upset, and to know I brought it on filled me with guilt. It was all I would need from her. "I'm getting thirsty," I said. "How about some tea?"

Grandmother smiled. "That sounds just fine. But I'll get it. You stay and keep working, dear."

"Thank you."

I began to plan my admission and barely heard her ask from the kitchen if I'd wanted cookies.

When she returned and we continued our projects, we turned silent. I thought about the asylum. It seemed like a wonderful place to stay for a spell. I could use somewhat of a holiday; time away to think in a pleasant environment.

CHAPTER NINE

I sat in front of the open window, the morning sun warm on my back. The air felt good, and I regretted missing a rare pleasant late summer day of clamming. It was early September and the season was dwindling. My nerves swirled in my stomach as I waited for Lester to come in from morning chores, anxious for his breakfast. I tried to concentrate on the birds chirping their early morning songs, but I got bored waiting and reread Nellie Bly. When I heard the door shut, I tucked the book under my leg and stared straight ahead as if I was sleeping with my eyes open. In my periphery, I saw Lester's shadow approach the table and then turn toward me.

"Pearl."

I stared at nothing.

"Pearl?" He stood in front of me and waved his hand in front of my face. A touch of panic crept into his voice. "Pearl, what's the matter?"

I slowly brought my eyes to his face and blinked dramatically. "Lester?"

"Where were you? How long have you been sitting here?"

"What…time…is it?"

"Nearly quarter til eight. Are you feeling poorly?"

I lay my flat palm on my collar bone. "I feel so hot. Dear me." Lester looked at me with a strange expression. Maybe that last 'Dear me' was too much. "I'm sorry. You must be starving. I'll get your breakfast right away." I pretended to try to stand up, but that my legs wouldn't hold me and I dropped back into the chair.

"Stay there. Let me get you some water."

When Lester turned his back to me to pump the water into a cup, I tossed Nellie Bly's book far under the Hoosier cabinet. Lester handed the cup to me and I drank slowly, allowing some to dribble down my chin. He gently wiped the mess away with his sleeve.

"Come lie down," he said, taking the cup from my hand and setting it on the floor. "Rest and I'll go get the doctor."

"I'll be alright. I think I just must be tired." I wasn't ready to put on my show for a doctor yet, though I knew I'd have to if I was going to get myself sent to the asylum.

I owed Jane a letter, so I snuck in some paper. I thought about it, but I couldn't tell Jane about my plans. She was too sensible and would've tried to stop me. When Lester and I first realized we had fallen in love, I mused with her about getting Lester to elope with me right away. Jane grabbed my forearms and shook me.

"Don't you dare!" she said. "You promised me I would be your witness at your wedding, and I promised you would be mine."

"I was thinking out loud."

"Well stop those thoughts right now. Besides, your father would break Lester's legs. And it would break your mother's heart. You know it's foolish."

"I know. I wasn't serious. Not really."

So I knew if I told Jane about my plan to get admitted to the asylum, an even more outrageous scheme, she would not react so calmly.

As I thought more about what Jane would say if I told her about my scheme, I somehow convinced myself that she would've been right.

I lost my nerves. Also, the clamming efforts became more feverish as we tried to accelerate the pace before winter came and the season was over.

One morning, we needed supplies for the clamming camp. I asked Lester if he could spare a little time to come with me to help me carry things, though I really wanted an excuse to spend time with him. We walked to the shops chatting about the recent clamming results. As much as he'd talked about the children we'd have one day when we were engaged, Lester avoided the subject now. I suppose, like me, he was embarrassed about what was keeping us from having children. I worried at times he would think the problem was him, and I didn't know how to tell him it wasn't.

Lester went to talk to the blacksmith about getting what he needed, and I went to Cady's for the dry goods. I had paid for my supplies and looked out the window for Lester. He said he'd only be a minute. He wasn't there, so I gathered up my packages in my arms, shifting to try and keep them from falling to the ground. I pushed my back end against the door to open it and stepped out into the bright sun. I looked left and right, no Lester, so I began walking toward the blacksmith.

I stepped around the corner to see Lester talking to a woman, Eleanor Lamphere. Eleanor used to clam with us when we were younger, but then she got too old and sophisticated. When she turned 18, she no longer clammed. I'd assumed she'd gotten married and moved away. Lester didn't notice me until I was about 20 feet away, and then he lurched toward me.

"Pearl!" He grabbed the packages from my arms. "You're done shopping already?"

"It's been half an hour," I said.

"Oh, I'm sorry. I ran into Eleanor and she was telling me all that she'd been up to lately."

I looked Eleanor up and down, noticing her fancy duds, too fancy for a random Tuesday at the blacksmith. I had no reason to be, but I was suspicious nevertheless, as I'd always sensed she'd had her sights on Lester, but he picked me.

"Well, I must be going," Eleanor said.

Lester nodded at her and smiled. I just nodded.

"It was nice chatting with you, Lester." She turned to face me. "It was nice seeing you again, too, Pearl." Then she added, a little too sweet to be genuine, "We should get together sometime."

"Certainly," I said, being as polite as possible.

For the entire way back to camp, I had to listen to Eleanor said this and Eleanor said that. Unfortunately, I was not surprised by Lester's naïveté. He was never one to notice when a girl was flirting with him.

A few weeks later, Lester's brother, Lyle, broke his leg and was stuck sitting in the house with his casted limb propped up on a chair and pillows. The harvest was coming in on the farm and couldn't wait. Their father, David, and uncle, Samuel, would help, but they still needed more hands, so instead of going to the clamming camp every day, Lester went the opposite way out of town to help on their family's farm.

I still helped with the cooking out and sorting, returning home every night. At first, I rushed home to fix Lester his supper, but when he returned home late saying his mother, Caroline, had already fed him, I stopped bothering. He started coming home later and later, occasionally even spending the night at his parents'. I knew better because I knew Lester and I trusted him, but I couldn't help remembering and remembering that day at the blacksmith with Eleanor. I became irrationally afraid if I didn't give Lester a child soon, I might lose him.

CHAPTER TEN

Though I awoke as usual, well before the late October fall sun began to show itself, I closed my eyes and stayed in bed, pretending to be asleep. I thought it would be difficult when Lester came in from the outhouse to see a dark, quiet kitchen. I braced myself for his questioning of why I wasn't needed to clam, but it never came. I don't even know if he noticed his coffee was unbrewed and his eggs still under the chickens. I must have dozed back off because I just heard the door latch as he left for the day for the farm. And then it occurred to me: I could be sick and Lester didn't even bother to check on me. I carried this frustration with me through the day as I ignored my duties and tried to immerse myself in *The Iron Heel* by Jack London, who turned out to be one of my favorite authors.

By dark, I was hungry, so I cooked supper – of eggs and fried ham – but Lester seemed to enjoy the change of pace rather than questioning my service of breakfast for supper. The third day, the mess began to grate on me and tried to call me away from my reading. It was almost as if I could see the dust particles piling one on top of another. I feared I was fulfilling my prophecy and actually going insane. I wanted a cup of tea but all of the cups were piled on the counter, so I had to wash a few to get me by. Though I began to question my sanity, I consoled myself by remembering that if I was truly insane, I wouldn't notice my boredom in being so unproductive.

Knowing the way to get a man's attention was through his stomach, I made an effort to have an early supper before Lester arrived home.

By Wednesday, I'd had enough. The bland soup I'd had waiting on the stove after I'd gone to my pretend slumber didn't help to catch

Lester's attention, so I didn't fix even that much. I thought of warming a pan of water as soup but decided I needed to take more aggressive action. I listened for Lester's footsteps and hugged the window, looking for his shadow to approach in the near full-moon light. I saw him and threw myself to the floor. I heard the doorknob turn and began my act.

"Where is it? Where did it go? Oh no!" I muttered as I frantically swept my arms under the furniture.

Lester squatted beside me. "Pearl, honey, what are you doing?"

I tried to make my eyes as blank as possible. Still on all fours, I looked up at him with confusion. I counted to three in my head. "I lost it," I said. "I've looked everywhere. I can't find it."

"Can't find what?"

"It's here somewhere. It's got to be." I returned to my flailing search.

"Tell me what it is, and I'll help you look."

What was it? I hadn't thought that far ahead, so I ignored him.

He took my left hand and felt down my ring finger. "It's not your ring," he said.

He got down on the floor and peered around next to me.

"Where was the last time you saw it?"

I swept my arm in a full circle. "Over there," I said.

Lester continued to search with me. I wondered how long I would have to continue, but it was only a couple of minutes before Lester sat up on his knees, watching me. I could see the look of bewilderment out of the corner of my eye. He raked his hand through his hair, and it stood up on end. Guilt set in. The poor man had been working all day in the field and now he was crawling around on the floor rather than washing up and filling his belly. I almost stopped, but then I remembered the children we would never have if I couldn't get myself figured out.

Finally, he grabbed my elbow. "Pearl," he said, pulling me from under the table. "Pearl!" I acted startled and gave him my attention. "Stop this, Pearl!" I crumpled my face, hoping I could force tears to come. "Why don't you go to bed?"

I shook my head. "I can't. I need to find it."

He let out a loud breath, no doubt the air he'd been holding since he'd walked in to find me having a fit on the floor in my nightgown.

He said, "I'll keep looking. As soon as I find it, I'll let you know."

I nodded my head as slowly as I could. "Al...right."

Lester pulled me to my feet and tucked me under the covers. He kissed my lips softly. "Go to sleep. I'll find it while you rest."

I closed my eyes. When I heard the door click, I opened them wide and let my pounding heart wash over me. He couldn't ignore me now. I had to pretend I was asleep again when he joined me a few hours later. When I heard his breath deep in sleep, I used the privy and found some old stale crackers to eat.

I thought I'd then be able to finally sleep, but I was wrong. I was unable to settle myself from my imagined distress. I was awake for hours even after Lester was snoring next to me.

CHAPTER ELEVEN

It wasn't necessary that I pretend to be asleep the next morning. It had taken me so long to fall asleep that I didn't feel the bed shift as Lester got up or hear the door latch as he left. I only saw the evidence of his taking charge of his own breakfast with an outline of fried egg still in the pan. And a note he left telling me to rest and not worry about his supper.

I sat down next to the window and started to read but soon grew bored. I needed to get myself into the asylum soon or I'd go mad with idleness. What could I do to accelerate my commitment? I decided to carry on with my charade of the missing mystery item. I devoted my time to the opposite of my daily duties.

I started with the bed. I had not made it anyway, but I carefully strewed the covers over the house. I turned my Sunday dress inside out and flung it over a chair. I emptied the cupboards of every dish and utensil and scattered them about the house. I only let myself break one cup that Lester had left over from his supply when we moved into the same household. I couldn't bear to break any of our treasured wedding gifts or my favorite pieces. I pulled every book from the bookcase, placing them open to various chapters. When I was finished, the place looked as if I'd been searching for a hair and searched every last nook and cranny in which it would fit in an attempt to find it.

I didn't want to repeat my frantic act from the day before, so I wondered, *How would a madwoman obsessed about finding a mystery object finally settle down and give up the fight? Whiskey.* I'd only enjoyed sips on Saturday nights with Lester and feared what I'd say if I'd actually imbibe on my own, so rather than consume any of the alcohol, I got rid of it by drizzling it in the grass. When I was done and the bottle was around one-third full, I set it on the counter, the cap askew. I felt terribly mean for wasting money in this way, something Lester was quite conscientious about, but I remembered in the long run how Lester would benefit.

Once I found out what I needed to know, I would be able to let Lester take me as a husband should his wife, and I would give him the baby we both needed.

I didn't want to see the look on Lester's face as the realization of his wife turning to insanity sunk further into his brain, so I went to bed while the sun was still up. Because of my late night and efforts undoing the house, I was able to fall asleep quite easily. I heard Lester come into the house and go from room to room, pausing for a few moments before investigating the next mess. I heard him in the kitchen area and knew he noticed the nearly empty and evaporating whiskey because he rushed to the bedside. He leaned down and sniffed my mouth. I hadn't thought of that detail; Lester must've been terribly confused.

I woke up the next morning late again, Lester already gone but after no apparent attempt to make himself breakfast. Everything was mostly back to its rightful place, except for a few misplaced dishes. I felt a rush of amusement at Lester's loving, but not quite on the mark, attempt to clean my mess. Then guilt engulfed me as I undid all of his work, repeating my activities from the day before. The practice made me more skilled at it so I was not tired when I finished. Amidst the housekeeping chaos, I sat with my book by the window again. I was turning the page when I saw someone walking toward the house. It was my mother. I raked my hands through my disheveled hair, threw down my book, and flung myself to my hands and knees.

I heard her knock but didn't respond. She knocked harder and I saw her try to look in through the window. We made eye contact, me on my hands in knees on the floor, she with a look of worry on her year-hardened face. She opened the door slowly and approached me like I was a rabid animal.

"Pearl, it's your mother. What are you doing?"

I danced around on all fours like a dog when its owner returns after a long time away. "I need to find it," I muttered.

"Find what?"

The conversation essentially took the same path as the one with Lester a couple of days prior. It ended the same way as well. My mother, obviously perplexed and out of ideas, put me to bed just as Lester had, squeezing my shoulder as she admonished me to stay there unless I had to use the privy.

"I'm going to get the doctor," she said as she backed out of the room.

I felt deep pangs of guilt for getting her dragged into my ruse, but there was nothing to be done about it.

When I knew she was gone, I tiptoed to get my book from where I had thrown it down. It took me several minutes to find my place in the story. I only got through two chapters when I heard the door open again and voices. I slid the book under my mattress, lay back into my pillows, and relaxed my eyes into a blank stare.

"Pearl, Dr. Swanson is here to help you."

The doctor sat on the edge of the bed. I turned my attention to him as slowly as I could.

"Your mother says you aren't yourself lately. She says you've been looking for something but you won't say what it is. Will you tell me? Perhaps I can help you find it."

I shook my head.

"We can't help you unless you tell us."

"Can't," I said, shaking my head again. It wasn't a lie. I couldn't tell him because I didn't know what it was. In a way, I was looking for my elusive child. That's what I'd thought about while turning everything inside out. I couldn't say it because I knew I couldn't physically find it that way, though, in a way, I suppose my actions were meant to help me find it indirectly and eventually.

Dr. Swanson sighed. "Let me take a look at you," he said. He listened to my back with his stethoscope. He put his fingers on my wrist to check my pulse. I tried to think of something frightening to get it racing, but I didn't know if I was successful. When he was done, he said, "Stay here and rest. I'm going to go out and talk to your mother."

I heard mumblings of their conversation but couldn't discern an intelligible word. Then all I heard was the clanking of items being returned to their rightful locations as my mother cleaned up my mess. Several times, I contemplated a miraculous recovery so my mother, her mind at ease, could return to her home, her duties, and the rest of my family. But then I thought of my lonely little house being forever absent of children and how my body or my mind would not allow me to complete the union required to conceive them and became more determined. I reasoned if she knew, my mother would thank me once she held her precious grandchild in her arms.

I watched the already shallow sunlight fade, dozing on and off, not daring to pull my book out from its hiding place when Mother could pop in at any moment. There were more mumblings when Lester returned home, then they cautiously entered the room, holding a dimly lit lantern close to my face. They spoke to me with the essence of their messages being if I didn't snap out of it, I would have to go away for a while to the asylum. The doctor had told them I had hysteria and that was the best cure. I almost giggled and clapped with glee that my scheme was working, but I stopped myself.

I turned toward them, and in a brief moment of clarity, said, "That might be best."

My mother got a stricken look on her face. She whispered, "But your father. You can't. He would disown you." I'd already thought of that but decided he'd forgive me once I was better. I wanted to tell my mother I wasn't really crazy, but I had to keep it to myself. I hoped it would all sink into the past once I knew the truth, then I could move away from it and give her grandchildren.

The next day, my mother sent my sister, Katherine, to sit with me. Lester told me she was coming and left me in bed until she arrived. Her startled look when she first laid her eyes on me almost made me laugh. I knew I looked a fright. I was a bit disappointed that she didn't tease me like we had been used to doing when we were young, especially since she was missing Camanche Mutual Improvement Association's Halloween party, but I suppose she was warned to be extra nice to me. Who knows what an insane person could do?

I watched her with my now usual blank eyes until she regained her composure. "Let's get you up and get you dressed," she said. She helped me into my everyday dress and brushed out my snarled hair. "Why don't we get you out of this bed?" Why is it when people treat adults like children, they use the inclusive pronoun as if they were in the same boat and somehow joining you in your predicament will somehow make it more palatable? She was being so nice to me that I didn't want to give her too much trouble, yet anyway.

I followed her to the sitting area, shuffling my feet. They scratched on the rough-hewn floors sending a shiver up my spine and producing goose pimples up and down my arms. She sat me in the rocking chair and then went back to make my bed. I craned my neck to watch her tucking the covers tightly under the straw tick mattress. She found the book I had hidden. She held it out to me. "Have you been reading this?" she asked. I stared past her. "Do you want to keep reading it?" She thrust it toward me, but I didn't respond.

"What about if I read it to you?" She crooked her index finger and used it to force me to turn my face toward hers. "Would you like that?" I nodded as slowly as I could. She pulled a chair over near me and sat down to read. She hadn't quite found the place where I had left off but I didn't say anything about the repeat chapter. Ever since I was a small child, I have found it difficult to focus my attention on words read aloud, so it was actually a blessing.

I was able to pay attention to my sister's reading for two chapters before my attention waned and I began to lose the story. I was afraid if I said something it would give away my true state of sanity, so I tried my best to put the blank bits together, but I couldn't, so I grew bored. I distracted myself by suddenly remembering that I was in a desperate search for some unknown item. I threw myself to the floor on all fours and muttered, "Where did it go? I must find it."

Mother or Lester must have warned her of my affliction because she didn't ask me what I was searching for, but gently and firmly grabbed my forearm and pulled me to my feet. She placed the book face-down on her chair and grabbed my shoulders.

She pushed me into the chair, saying, "We'll look for it later. I'm too engrossed in this story to put it down now, aren't you? Let's finish the chapter and then I'll help you look for it."

This actually helped because she went back to the beginning of the chapter to start reading. She thought I hadn't noticed when she started a new chapter or that I hadn't remembered she said she'd help me look for my precious lost item because she kept reading until I lost my place and started the charade all over again. We passed the entire morning this way. After she fed me the food my mother had sent with her, she lay me down for a nap. I thought about repeating my hunting performance from the morning, but I was tired of that. Instead I lay in my bed replaying every moment I had spent with my Great Uncle Mason in my mind, trying to remember something, anything, that would tell me if I was blocking from my memory something dreadful that had happened to me. Nothing other than those two instances and that feeling of terror that gripped me whenever I knew he was in my vicinity came to my mind.

CHAPTER TWELVE

On Tuesday, we left in the predawn dark. The leaves wet and thick on the ground from heavy rain and winds the last two days, making an odor of spent tea. I made my way to the carriage to which Lester had the team hitched and poised, shuffling my feet through the thick fallen leaves like I'd done at my grandma's when I was a girl. These were some of the only times I forgot myself in my senses and didn't keep a vigil eye out for a lurking Great Uncle Mason. But, this time, they were too wet and just slapped against my boots, some sticking to them, like bright yellow bits of wallpaper standing out on the black leather.

I hoisted myself into the carriage, seating myself next to Lester and tucking blankets around my legs and up to my chin to keep warm. Lester had already secured my one bag. I remembered how he used to hold my hand to help me into the carriage and wondered if it was his realization I hadn't needed his help, the length of our marriage wearing, or the fact that I'd failed to give him any children that left him sitting, staring straight ahead, waiting for me.

The sky brightened as we drove, but it was still dark and cloudy. When we'd pass a farmstead, Lester would slow the horses so their hooves wouldn't slip too much on the oily, wet leaves drifted on the road. The tree limbs were mostly bare except for a few that dangled and then let loose. I watched them float and then land with a sea of others. I could feel my cheeks chilling, but it felt good, the cool. I wished the sun would come out, but it refused. I knew if it did, the putrid golden brown would look more brilliant. But I suppose being too cheerful would've confused the reason for the trip, so the deep clouds were better suited to helping me maintain my ruse.

We reached town at about noon. We drove through the main street, past the shops and restaurants. There were two hotels, both two stories high, but one with a couple of scantily clad ladies holding shawls around their bare shoulders hanging off the upper balcony. The smells coming from the restaurants made my stomach growl and I longed for Lester to take me into one, not only to eat but perhaps to spend a few more minutes with me before beginning our separation. But I knew my hopes were in vain. My mother, without Father's knowledge, had packed us a lunch which Lester would never waste, and he had work to get home to so couldn't take the time for an elongated meal. Besides, how could he know I would not make a scene in my insane state? So we rode past, me taking in all the sights and sounds and Lester watching only the other carriages and a few autos, trying to negotiate safely. The autos were a sight and I hoped the day would come when I could take another ride in one, speeding along the Mississippi River, tasting accelerated freedom. Lester saw them only as a nuisance, something to scare his horses and send them into a careening panic. They were getting more reasonably priced. But they were still too much for Lester who said he'd heard anyone who'd known anyone who had one complained about all the repairs they needed and how they became stuck in the slightest road mud.

The asylum was located about a mile outside of town on top of a gentle rise. It was a huge building, like the European castles I'd seen in book drawings. Corinthian columns combined with arches to create an open-walled square room leading to the front door. The foundation was made of prairie granite, and the walls were built of tan-colored, almost blond blocks, likely limestone from a local quarry. The tallest, main part of the wide building had an Italianate style toward the tip and ornate awnings shaded some of the windows. The lawn was sprawling and green with trees whose leaves would look enchanting when the sun hit them, I knew. I couldn't wait to walk among them, breathing in the fresh air.

"Whoa!" Lester pulled under the open-walled area at the top of a circle drive. "Eastern Iowa Asylum for the Insane" was chiseled into the stone above the entrance. I sat in the carriage as close to the side as I could get without falling out, my arms clutching my own body in a tight hug, staring straight ahead, my mind whirring but trying to not to let it show in my eyes. I tried not to cry as Lester came from behind the carriage and opened my door. He picked me up like I'd imagined he would the babies we were supposed to have and brought me inside. I left my blankets, mistakenly thinking I wouldn't need them. The foyer was bright with windows stretching nearly from ceiling to floor. A grand staircase with dark wood railings led to the second floor. Fancy plaster medallions decorated the ceiling. It smelled medicinal, a sharp odor that stung my nose. I didn't know if insane people would notice, so I swallowed a sneeze, which came out as a small choke. Lester deposited me on a mattress on top of a table with wheels. I curled up as tight as I could. Two men dressed in white pushed some sort of levers with their feet and wheeled me down the hallway. I shut my eyes tight and put my hands over my ears to try to muffle the moans and screams coming from behind the thick doors with small windows.

They stopped in front of an open door and used their feet again to engage what I'd realized were wheel locks.

"Are you able to stand, Mrs. Sinkey?"

I looked up and nodded. Each grabbed an elbow and helped me to stand. My limbs had been so tensed up, I swayed involuntarily, and they guided me to a chair.

Lester signed several papers. He then handed my bag to a woman dressed in all white, kissed my lips quickly, and wrapped his arms around me. I pressed in to enjoy him holding me, but he pulled away too quickly.

"It's a long way back," he said. I nodded. He said, "I love you."

I said, "I love you, too." And then he was gone. Leaving me alone with my insanity.

As I was guided to my room on the Fifth Ward, I tried to peer into all the rooms we passed, shuffling my feet to slow down. As I passed one room, the door swung open, banging against the outer wall, and a man, also dressed in all white, rushed out of the room. I was able to glimpse in to see cabinets that I assumed held the files. At least now I knew where to begin my search. I quickly learned, however, that the door to the room was always locked and it was rarely unoccupied.

The attendant gripping my elbow between his thumb and index finger led me to my room at the end of a long hall. He opened the door and pointed to the bed where a set of clothes lay waiting for me. He still held my bag, but as I went to take it from him, he pulled it roughly away and held it to his chest. It was the last time I'd see it during my stay.

"When you are dressed, open the door and place the clothes you're wearing neatly in the hallway. A doctor will be in to see you shortly."

I lifted the flimsy material and pulled the gown over my head. I knew I would freeze and hoped they'd let me have the sweater I'd packed. When I was dressed and placed the clothes I had worn in outside the door as I was told, I sat on the bed, pulling my knees to my chest under the fabric to attempt to warm them. I waited and thought of ways I could get into the record room I'd seen.

After what seemed like over an hour – I couldn't tell because there were no clocks – an orderly came to take me to the file room I'd seen. A doctor came in. His grey hair was messy, like he'd scratched his head too many times. His bloodshot eyes were kind but preoccupied. He asked me if I knew what I was doing there.

"Yes," I said. "My family was concerned about me and thought it would be helpful for me to get away for a while."

"And you agreed with them?"

"I have been out of sorts lately, so I didn't disagree with them."

"You are here willingly then?"

"Yes."

"Your husband told us that you had been frantically searching for something in the house but were unable to find it and wouldn't tell them what it was. Can you tell me what you were looking for?"

I pulled my face into a confused expression. "Looking for something? I don't remember looking for anything. I had been doing a lot of deep cleaning the last bit of time. My family told me the rest I would receive here would revive my mood."

"That it shall. Is there anything else you'd like to talk about?"

"Do you know a Mason Hazelton?"

"No. Should I?"

"He was a patient here years ago. I just wondered if you knew him."

"Are you concerned you somehow obtained your condition from him?"

"No. He was in the war between the states and just couldn't seem to get over it."

"Why do you ask about his time here?"

I couldn't think of a good answer.

As they "settled me in and told me the rules," I looked around the stark room. The white walls loomed, interrupted only by tall windows. Cabinets lined the walls. The orderly turned to one behind her, opened a drawer, and removed a stack of papers. *That must be where they keep the records*, I thought. Once all was in order, the orderly stuffed the papers into a folder.

"I'll show you back to your room now," she said as cheerfully as if this were a posh hotel I was visiting for a holiday.

She squeezed my elbow and guided me to the door. Once we were in the hallway, she kept tight hold of it while she locked the file room door with one of the many keys hanging on a hoop she pulled from her pocket. How would I ever get in there?

Over the next few days, I would study that room as closely as I could, peering in every time I walked by. If there wasn't someone in there, it seemed like the door was always locked. The only way in would be to get ahold of the key, but I didn't know how I could figure which was the correct key, so I'd have to get ahold of the whole set.

I was preoccupied with the harsh reality of what I had gotten myself into. There were more stark, white walls in the room I would share with three other patients, not knowing at the time it was a temporary residence until I received my own room. The tall windows that looked cheery from the outside were barred like a jail cell on the inside. By the time my paperwork was completed and I was checked in, it had been too late for supper, so I was given a weak cup of broth and buttered bread while waiting. Within minutes after arriving in my room, the other three patients arrived and it was time for bed. We were told to place our clothing on a chair after changing into our nightgowns, which were removed and placed in the hallway. As soon as we were in bed, the door was closed and locked from the outside.

My roommates didn't talk to each other or to me. I shivered on top of the oilcloth and under the thin sheet and worn black wool blanket covers on my bed, unable to sleep. After a while, I was glad the door had been locked as, in the distance, I heard shrieks and screams. I had finally started to drift off at what had to be after or close to 2 a.m. when an attendant shone a lantern into the room, waving it around to see every corner, bringing me back to wide awake. The light through the windows was showing its first hint of the day to come when I began to doze again but was awakened by one of the other patients in the room wandering in circles around the beds.

CHAPTER THIRTEEN

We were awakened at 6 a.m. with the door banging against the wall and our clothes slapping against the floor as they were flung back into the room from the hallway.

"Put them on," the attendant demanded, a scowl imprisoning her face. Our attire consisted of an underskirt made of rough dark cotton; the cheap, white calico shirt was sewn onto the putrid brown skirt in one piece.

We were allowed to use the water closet and rinse off our faces with plain, cold water. All nearly four dozen of us on the hall used the same two towels. Breakfast at seven consisted of muddy tea and a cup of oatmeal gruel. I wondered when the wonderful meals my grandmother described would be served. Everyone sitting at the long tables looked the same, all with the same worn, thin clothes, straggly hair, and blank faces. After breakfast, my nails were trimmed until the soft undersides bled out and then I was questioned by a doctor. At noon, we were served a bit of cold meat and potato. After this meager dinner, except for another interrogation session with the doctor, we sat all afternoon, quietly and with no amusement until four when we were dressed in tattered hats, hoods, and shawls from the last century and taken outside. Our excursion was accomplished in a single file line on the paths that meandered through the expansive garden. We were not allowed on the grass. Those who got out of the line were swatted back into formation. We passed a group of at least 50 women who were maintained in their line by a long rope attached to wide belts around their waists. Behind them and which they pulled like a pack of oxen, was a heavy iron cart with two women riding in it. Our evening meal consisted of a cup of weak tea – a nice change from the muddy version of the morning, though I thought perhaps they could've evened them out – and bread spread with bitter butter, which no woman I knew would be willing to put her name on. Talking was prohibited so we couldn't even distract ourselves, forced to choke down this "food" in silence.

I took tiny bites of the bread, eating the bottom away from the butter, to try to make it last as the most palatable selection available. After each bite, I sipped the tea to wash its dry texture down so it wouldn't scratch my throat. I was about halfway through when I set the bread down to reach for my tea and I saw what looked like a black string poking out. I picked it up to examine it, pulling the bread away from the black thing. It only took a fraction of a second to realize it was a spider. I let out a guttural scream and threw it down. My tablemates stared at me in startled attention, but the attendants on duty hadn't seemed to notice. I raised my hand to get one's attention. I waved it around before one saw me and came over.

"What!" The attendant was obviously annoyed at the interruption.

I pointed at the bread. "There's a spider in my bread."

She picked it up and held it a few inches in front of her eyes. "Huh," she said before walking away.

I had lost my appetite anyway and fought to keep what I'd already swallowed in my stomach, but she didn't bring me a replacement. After that, I examined everything placed in front of me before putting a bite into my mouth.

I quickly found out that all of the best provisions were saved for the doctors, nurses, and attendants. They ate an array of fresh fruit, white bread, and nice meats. I wondered how the doctors could allow all of this to happen under their leadership. But then I figured it out: they didn't know.

That evening as all of the patients sat in the parlor, a few them stood up and started to dance to songs they sang. I held my breath as I waited for the attendants to put an angry stop to the behavior, but to my amazement, the attendants stayed away. Shortly, the doctors arrived and joined in. Then most of the other patients, smiling and laughing, started singing and dancing as well. It was the first, and as I would soon experience, the only joyful times that happened, except when someone was discharged home.

I tapped my toes but felt too shy to join in, not sure what was expected of me or if the others would accept me.

A girl with oak colored hair sitting next to me leaned toward me and whispered in a flat tone, "Why don't you join them?"

"Oh no, that's alright. I enjoy watching," I said, turning towards her to make eye contact and perhaps a friend. But her face held a scowl like I'd never seen while her body was slumped as sullenly as a child who'd dropped his candy in the dirt.

"It's all a big lie, anyway," she said. "The nurses and attendants have the doctors so fooled, they are as delusional as some of the patients."

Despite her demeanor, my curiosity got the best of me. "What do you mean?"

"If you tell a doctor that one of them hit you or taunted you, they will just tell the doctor that you were imagining things. And who's the doctor going to believe? Them, of course. They aren't going to believe an insane person over them. Then, when the doctors aren't looking, you'll be punished." She held her arm out to show me a long, thin scar from the space between her middle and ring fingers to her thumb. "You learn fast to keep your mouth shut. As far as the doctors know, this happened when I got hold of a knife I wasn't supposed to have."

I didn't know what to say. I kept thinking, *What have I gotten myself into?* My feet were still as I continued to watch the singing and dancing, realizing with dread that I'd made a mistake.

CHAPTER FOURTEEN

I'd never experienced time passing so slowly, even as a little girl waiting for Christmas morning. When that first Sunday, visiting day, arrived, it felt like months had passed rather than days. I'd already given up on my quest and resigned myself to the fact that if I was ever going to know what happened to me, it would come from unlocking my own mind. There was no way I'd ever get a look at those files, assuming Great Uncle Mason's were even in there, as my meager math skills told me that room would never hold every patient's file for all time. I tried to not dwell on my stupidity and just concentrate on the future and getting out. I was tempted to tell the doctors of my real troubles, but I was afraid my incarceration in the cold, hard, white prison would be cemented, and I would never get out. I was determined that Lester would take me home that day, and if I couldn't open myself up to my wifely duties, I would pretend, hoping that at least I would eventually not feel split in two every time.

Before visiting day arrived, though, we had to be bathed. I thought that at least this Saturday night ritual would be like home. But other than the occurrence of the bath, it was nothing like home, and not just because of the lack of whiskey.

With several patients in the room watching, we were plunged in ice-cold water and scrubbed with soft soap. It was the first time that week I'd seen soap and the only times I would during my entire stay. To rinse, the attendants poured three buckets of nearly frozen water over my head. I was barely dabbed with an already wet towel which had been used on the bathers before me, and, dripping wet, they yanked a flannel gown over my head that proclaimed our location in big, black letters, "Lunatic Asylum, EIA, H2," as if someone would forget where we were. Or maybe it was so we could be returned should we find a way to escape. I was a couple of dozen deep in the line and became more and more disgusted as the tub water was used over and over until it was thick, like sediment-filled river water. Then they would let it run out and refill the tub without washing it, plunging in woman after woman, some with skin eruptions. I tried to calculate how many bathers came through the tub before it was drained and refilled, but there didn't seem to be any rhyme or reason. They didn't comb our hair until the next day, so it was so snarled I'd almost wished they'd just cut it off.

Lester had promised me he would be there to visit me, but I knew not to expect him early because he'd have chores to do and then he'd have the long journey. I prepared what I would say in my head so as not to waste time. I knew, also, that he wouldn't be able to stay long.

After my scant dinner, I was met in the dining room door by an attendant holding a sweater and a different dress.

"Put this on." She crossed her arms in front of her chest as I slipped the dress over my head and put my arms into the sweater sleeves. "Button it." My fingers were numb from cold. I did my best to push the pearl discs through the holes of the beige sweater from memory. I thought about the happy days clamming along the river and became anxious about getting out and warm weather. When I got to the bottom of buttoning the sweater, I realized I'd misaligned the buttons, but before I could correct them, the attendant sighed loudly and slapped my hands away.

"Here, let me," she said. "There's not time for this. Visiting hours only last so long."

So Lester was there. I stood with my arms hanging limp at my sides, willing the tears to stay in my throat. Tears seemed to be an invitation from the attendants for mocking and laughter. Plus I didn't want Lester to see anything that may cause him to think I still belonged there.

The attendant grabbed my elbow, swung me around, and steered me toward the visiting parlor. This model ward, reserved only for visitors, was close to the middle area of the building referred to as Central Main where all of the administrative offices were located, including the heavily guarded file room. It was well furnished, organized, and clean. The diners luxuriated with tablecloths, napkins, and a complete array of cutlery, silver spoons, forks, and knives. All of the wards housed a parlor, dining room, clothes room, bathtub room, water closet, laundry chute, and attendants' rooms, but they were much more sparsely furnished with much less comfortable pieces.

By then I was at least given my own room, having proved my worth to be promoted from the disturbed ward to the second ward where I was allowed to recover from the 2 a.m. lantern check by the night watch until 8 a.m.

Lester sat on one of the velvet-plush chairs, his hat in his hands. My heart jumped when I saw him, just like it did those years ago when I saw him skipping rocks on the banks of the river. He stood when he saw me. I walked to him and he kissed me lightly on the lips. We sat next to each other like awkward courters unsure of what to say.

I smiled my brightest and broke the silence. "I'm well now, Lester. I know you aren't able to stay long, so if you just get my things we can go home."

His face lit up. "That's wonderful. The house has become a shambles and I haven't eaten decently all week. But are you sure you've recovered?"

"Oh, yes, the rest has done me wonders. I'm sorry that I put you through such a fright. I'm certain I'm over all of that now and will be happy getting back to cooking, keeping house … and my other … duties … er, activities."

Lester patted my knee and rose. He seemed to glide to the supervising attendant. He waved at me while she left him, returning several minutes later with one of the doctors, who took Lester to one of the back offices. I waited with my hands in my lap, perched on the chair's edge. After even more minutes had passed, I sat back deep into the cushion. My eyelids were getting heavy and I could barely hold them open. Since I'd been there, I hadn't been able to sleep a wink at night, but I seemed to doze off every time I sat down during the day.

The door opened and I saw Lester following one of the doctors, who glared at me before turning back to the asylum's belly. Lester looked grim. I thought that perhaps they'd lost my things since he wasn't carrying my bag. He didn't sit next to me, but stood in front of me, staring above my head out the window. I stood up so he couldn't avoid looking at me.

"I spoke with the doctor. He and the other doctors feel like you aren't ready to leave quite yet."

"Why?"

"He said that you've actually worsened. That you are in denial of your … condition."

I shook my head. "I'm not in denial; I'm fine. I came here voluntarily, which means I can leave anytime I want to."

"I suppose, but I think you should stay a while longer. Just until the doctors say for sure that you've recovered."

"But I am recovered."

Lester pushed his hair back off his forehead and pushed his hat onto his head. "The doctors are experts, and they say that one of the greatest signs someone is truly sick is that they insist that they are not. Once you admit your illness and recover, they will release you to go home."

Another week. I could endure another week if it meant that it would give Lester peace of mind that I'd completely recovered. I would simply tell the doctors that I knew I'd been insane, that I was looking for something I couldn't name, but I knew now that it was my mind playing tricks on me and I wasn't going to look for it any longer.

"Alright, I'll stay."

As Lester hugged me, he said, "I'll be back to visit in a few weeks."

I pulled away from him. "Why won't you come next Sunday?" I asked.

"By the time I can get here, we only have a short time together before it's time to leave again. It's not worth it. If I wait a few weeks, I can save up enough to stay at the hotel on Friday and Saturday nights so we can spend the entire day together. Won't that be better?"

I nodded my head. It was logical, of course, but I still felt wounded that it wasn't worth a long trip to spend just a short time with me. I would've traveled around the world to spend an hour with Lester.

Three weeks passed and Lester, true to his word, came to visit, staying in the hotel in town on Friday and Saturday nights. We seemed more like strangers than husband and wife. Our conversation was strained.

I made the mistake of asking him about Thanksgiving.

"It was good," he said. "Everyone missed you, of course, but Mother had the usual big spread. I swear the turkey was as big as the table." He laughed, cupping his hands and spreading his arms to demonstrate. "And, of course, the girls baked one of about every pie you can imagine." When he finally turned to look at me, I must've had a pained expression. He said, "It was alright. The turkey was dry, though, not like your mother's."

I smiled meekly.

"What about you? Did they have a big dinner?"

I hesitated, wondering if I should tell him the truth. That what they called turkey could've been fish or pork because it all tasted like compressed sawdust. That the potatoes where cold and mashed just meant the potatoes looked like they had been stepped on instead of delivered whole like usual. That instead of pie, we got a ginger molasses cookie we could've used for a hammerhead. I settled on, "It was alright."

He told me all about his work but would not say anything about my return home. For fear of a repeat from the last time, I kept my mouth quiet as well. I thought my release was imminent until suddenly Lester was gone, and I realized he hadn't mentioned returning. I knew work at the cutting factory would be beginning soon, so I dared not hope for an extended visit. And seeing I wasn't worth the trip for a short duration, I didn't expect to see my husband until I could convince the doctors to recommend my release and I could send for him to retrieve me. I knew by then my father had to have learned where I was, and I knew he'd prohibit any visits from my family. I resigned myself to facing the loneliness.

*****

The next day, after asking for pencil and paper, receiving two sheets and a stub I had to keep turning to try to keep the tip useful, I wrote a letter to Jane, telling her of my plight and asking her to help me. I tried to be patient waiting for a return letter as the cold intensified and I could scarcely remember what it felt like to have warm feet, but as each day after the first two weeks passed, I became more and more despondent. I resigned myself to the fact that Jane hadn't believed the assertion of my sanity and didn't want to become involved. I didn't know how I'd survive the three years I'd learned was the length of a stay before patients were released or sent to the incurable asylums.

I worked hard to keep my current position and strived to be moved to the first ward where the convalescing and soon to be released patients were housed. When patients became disruptive, they were secured away from the other patients, often violently, by the attendants. Those who were most violent were sent to wards seven, eight, or nine, but frequently, their most violent behavior was trying to escape or sneak out letters.

I saw one patient punished by an attendant dragging her across the floor by her arm and foot. They pulled another patient's hair out. I overheard conversations of patients talking about other patients fastened with straps or mufflers with long sleeves that could be tied under the bed, heads being knocked against the wall for not taking their medication. The first night I was there, I was given medication to help me sleep, but it did the opposite and gave me a headache. From then on, I avoided doing or saying anything that may make it seem like I needed medicinal treatment.

One day, the young woman with the oak colored hair from the first night of singing and dancing, who I'd noticed cycled between bouts of energy, asking to help clean or do anything to help the attendants and intense sadness or prolonged periods of apathy and crying, talked to me in low whispers as we waited for admittance to the dining room.

"My name's Sarah," she said, no longer scowling and sullen. "What's yours?"

"Pearl."

"At first, I didn't think you belonged here, but I've noticed lately you've seemed to become sadder and sadder," she said.

I nodded. "I don't belong here, but my husband believes the doctors who say I do. I wrote my best friend to ask her to help me get out, but she hasn't written back. It's been almost a month."

"Did you write that in your letter?"

I lifted my head to look at her and saw bright blue eyes behind the straw-like hair that fell in front of them.

"Didn't you know that they read all of the letters that come in or out?" she asked.

I shook my head.

"They do, and if there's anything they don't like in them, they throw them away."

That must be it, I thought. I would have to find another way. It occurred to me that it didn't seem like Sarah belonged there either. As I opened my mouth to ask her about it, I noticed an attendant glaring our way, so I snapped my mouth closed and hung my head to again stare to at the dirt-crusted linoleum.

After between a half and three-quarters of an hour of waiting, we were finally allowed into the dining room for our dinner. I was so hungry, I thought perhaps the food might be acceptably palatable. I was mistaken. The receptacles which had held our tea that morning were now filled with a barren soup, and a plate next to it held one small, cold, boiled potato and a greenish tinted piece of beef. Again, there were no knife or fork to cut it.

The next day, I asked again for a pencil and paper to write Jane another letter. This time I began by reminding her of that special game we used to play when we were kids and said I wanted to play it again. The game was a means of communicating that only she and I knew about. It was a way we could talk about the boys we liked in school without anyone knowing about whom we discussed.

The weeks passed and still, no letter from Jane arrived. Lester, not much inclined to the written word, sent short notes reporting on the happenings at home, as bland and distancing as you can imagine. Sarah and I became closer. I learned that her peaks of energy came from when she thought she could get the attendants on her side to help get her released by being helpful and of service. Her desperate sadness and crying came from the letters she received from her estranged husband detailing all she was missing from her son's life and threatening that she would never see him again. The doctors characterized the behavior as more evidence of her insanity.

In mid-December, I had my first and only real clash with an attendant. As we patients sat shivering in the desolate parlor for the afternoon like usual, I watched the snow, the first one of the season to stick, fall softly in giant flakes. As I watched them float and grab hold of the bare tree limbs outside the window, I counted the months on my fingers. February. March. April. May. … October. November. If I'd not failed myself and my husband, I could've been holding our child in my arms rather than clutching them around my middle to keep them warm. I suddenly became inconsolably homesick. I first tried to hold in my tears; when that didn't work, I tried to keep them silent, but before I knew what was happening, I was sobbing, loudly.

One of the attendants stomped to me and stood, her toes pointed outward, and her thick arms sticking out at right angles as she held her hands on her hips. "Stop that!"

I looked up at her. Her face, stretched by her hair pulled tight into a bun at the back of her head, was blurry.

"I … I just …"

"I didn't ask! Just stop it!"

I swallowed. My saliva caught in my throat and I started choking. I wheezed as I tried to catch my breath. The attendant grabbed my hair and pulled me to my feet. I gagged as the choking intensified. I thought that was what it must feel like to be drowning. I held my breath, but it didn't help. She dragged me across the room and out into the hall. I was afraid I would vomit my dinner, but I never did. Not that it would've looked any different than it had before it went in.

Shoving me into a closet, she said, "Stay there until you stop making such a racket. If you don't, we'll have to give you a treatment." As she said, "treatment," she sneered. I already knew she meant one of the inhumane restraining devices; I'd seen the "treatment" before.

I sunk to the floor in the dark. The only light came from the sliver of space underneath the door. As my eyes adjusted, I looked around but saw nothing. The closet seemed to serve no other purpose than the one for which I was there. I huddled toward the back, folding my legs up under my skirt to try to warm them. I concentrated on my breathing. In. Out. In. Out. It finally slowed into a regular rhythm, though the tears still slid. I wiped them away with my sleeve, which got it wet, which made me even colder.

I couldn't tell how long I was in there. I turned and leaned my head against the wall. I had started to doze when the door swung open. I put up my arm to shield my eyes from the harsh light. The same attendant who'd put me there stood in the same stance, though all I could see this time was her dark shadow.

I waited.

"Well!" she said.

I stood.

"Go!" she said more like a bark from the most ferocious guard dogs back home.

I shuffled past her and joined the line moping its way to the dining room. Sarah appeared behind me.

"Are you alright?" she asked.

I nodded, too afraid to say anything more.

She squeezed my arm. "You need to get out of here."

I didn't have to answer.

CHAPTER FIFTEEN

Christmas morning. It had me glum and still desperately homesick. After a breakfast of gravy, potatoes, and bread, some of the patients got to leave with their families on day passes. I'd written to Lester to tell him that I could leave on a pass for the holiday, but he replied regretfully, saying that there wasn't enough time to get me, bring me home, and take me back all in one day. And we couldn't afford for him to stay at a hotel. So I, with many more who couldn't leave, were stuck. In a feeble effort to cheer those of us who couldn't leave, the attendants brought us packages and letters sent by family and friends.

They called our names, and one by one, we collected our gifts.

"Pearl Sinkey."

I was surprised that there was something for me. Though I'd written to my family and Jane numerous times, the only thing I'd received back were newspaper style letters that my mother snuck out, reporting on what was happening at home. I imagined that my letters had been diverted from them because I'd not said what the doctors wanted me to, so they were likely angry at me for not reaching out to them.

I unwrapped the package, carefully releasing the folded paper edges. Tears filled my eyes as I poured over the contents. My sisters had embroidered a beautiful handkerchief adorned with tiny lilacs, my favorite flower. From my mother, there were freshly knitted socks that I immediately put on my frozen feet and plotted to hide so they wouldn't be taken from me. My brother, John Junior, sent a cat figurine whittled out of driftwood. This, with its sharp edges, I knew would be taken away, so I tucked it into my dress and let it slip partway into my drawers until I could hide it in my room. I was amazed that the packages hadn't already been opened and these things removed. Perhaps it was the holiday spirit, but more likely it was laziness.

My mother had also written a short note. It read, "Grandma Hailey sends her love. She wanted to write herself, but she has been very ill lately. I hope you make it home to see her one last time."

The tears now flowed freely. My mother's note was cold and sharp, like it had cut my heart wide open. It was clear that they were angry with me. I clasped my hands behind my head and buried my head in my lap. I felt someone sit down next to me. I flinched and held in my breath, not letting it out until I felt a consoling palm on my hands. I uncurled and saw Sarah.

"Hello," I said, wiping my tears with my dress sleeve, which was really too thin to soak up anything. "Merry Christmas."

"What is it, Pearl?"

I couldn't speak so I handed her the note.

"I'm so sorry," she said. She pointed at the embroidery. "That's beautiful."

I sniffed my nose to pull in its secretions; I didn't want to wipe that on my dress. "Thank you. My sisters made it for me."

"How nice. Did you get anything else?"

For some reason, I trusted Sarah's warm brown eyes. I looked around to make sure no one was watching and showed her my socks. I whispered, "My brother also whittled me a cat, but I can't show it to you." I pointed at my waist and we both stifled giggles.

"Did your family send anything?" I asked.

She shook her head.

"I'm sorry. Maybe they didn't get it in the post in time and it'll arrive soon."

"No," she said, "that's not it." I could tell she was doing her best to hold back tears. "They don't want anything to do with me."

It was my turn to attempt to comfort her. I patted her hands folded in her lap. "I'm sure that's not it. You said that they don't send our letters. I know that's why my family is angry with me. Maybe it's the same for you. It's just a misunderstanding."

She shook her head again. "It's my husband. He has them believing I'm incurably mad and afraid that since they are my blood relatives, they are susceptible to the madness as well."

"Are you sure?"

"He visited me once after I'd been here for two months and told me."

"Why would he do that?"

"My husband is a pastor, and I disagreed with him at a bible class. I expressed an opinion that conflicted with the Creed of the Presbyterian Church. He took it as a personal attack. He said he was disgraced. He told me if I didn't take it back, I would be sorry. I couldn't imagine what he could do. And once I had said it, I didn't think anyone would believe me if I had tried to take it back. He had me committed."

"That's terrible." She had told me her husband had her committed, but I hadn't heard a reason why before. I squeezed her hands. I wanted to hug her but I didn't dare.

She could no longer hold in her tears. "Isaac is five now. I haven't seen him since he was four."

I wrapped my arms around her, damning whatever consequences may come. I needn't have worried. All of the nurses were gone, no doubt enjoying the holiday pastries the local bakery had sent over that I saw them sneak past the dining room into the first ward dining prep areas. I held Sarah until she pushed me away.

"I'm alright now," she said. "Thank you. I better stop this or I'll get in trouble."

I laughed in spite of myself. "It's ridiculous. We're the supposed insane imprisoned here and we aren't allowed to cry."

Sarah smiled and then broke out into her own laughter. "You're right. It's absurd."

We settled back quietly. I placed the lilac embroidered handkerchief in Sarah's lap. "Here," I said, "you have that."

She held it toward me. "No, I couldn't. Your sisters made that especially for you."

I pushed her hand away, refusing to take the piece back. "Then consider it a loan. You just hold onto it for me, and whenever you get out of here or I get out of here, I'll take it back then. Alright?"

"Alright. Thank you."

As I watched her run her index finger over the lavender and green stitches, I wished that somehow I could help Sarah get out of the asylum and get her son back.

New Year's came nearly the same as Christmas, without the gifts. For dinner, we received what they said was mutton, bread, potatoes, and white winter radishes. January held many days of bitter cold, but there wasn't much snow. A few flakes every now and again, but nothing that coated the ground. My main focus for the entire month was to try to get warm.

I wrote to Jane again to ask if she could tell me anything about Lester since he hadn't replied to my letters. My fruitless efforts to find out if Mason had done anything terrible to me left me feeling that my whole life was slipping away. I'd decided I needed to get out of the asylum, but I didn't know how. I hadn't thought that far ahead when I'd determined to get myself in. I tried to behave like a normal, sane person, but they didn't believe me. It seemed pretending was a common tactic the mad used when trying to get out of their predicaments in the asylum. I feared the reason I hadn't heard from Lester was because they weren't sending my letters, so, despite our secret code, I used my neighbor's name as the return address and slipped my letter into her pile of outgoing mail. She seemed to have at least one visitor every visiting day, so I hoped that meant they were sending her letters. I addressed it to "Janey Jo," hoping Jane would recognize my childhood nickname for her and open the letter from her "Pearly Pea."

After dinner on the first Sunday of February 1909, the 7th, an orderly approached me, pinched my bent elbow, and guided me toward the visiting area outside. It was still winter but the lack of snow and warm temps of the previous week teased with a hint of spring, so visitors were taking advantage in the courtyard where roses bloomed profusely in the summer and a fountain flowed, which meant to provide an illusion of the pleasantness inside. But the roses' pink shades were a stark contrast to the cold white of the walls, floors, and ceiling where we spent most of our time. I wasn't expecting any visitors, though since I hadn't heard anything from Lester in weeks, I hoped with all my heart it was him. But I came around the corner and saw Jane, standing, her hands clenched in front of her protruding stomach like she was in pain.

When I got within 20 feet, she ran to me, holding her skirt off the ground. "Pearl! You're alright." She pulled me to her and hugged tight. I had to hunch over somewhat to make room for her belly. "I came as soon as I could," she said. "I'm so sorry. I had no idea."

I led Jane as far away from prying ears as I could. "Thank you so much for coming," I whispered. "I didn't know what else to do."

We sat on a marble bench behind a bare rose bush. I lay my head on Jane's shoulder, and she put her arm around me. She whispered, "You need to get out of here, Pearl, and get back to Lester."

Her urgency alarmed me. I snapped up and looked at her face. She pressed my head back to her shoulder. "Shhh. Don't draw any attention." I relaxed into her, my heart pounding.

"What's happened? Is Lester ill?"

"It's that Eleanor. She's been spending a lot of time with Lester. She told me she's planning to get him to leave you and be with her."

"Why would she tell you that?"

Jane didn't respond, so I sat up to find tears in her eyes. She sighed.

"I'm so sorry, Pearl. I was angry when you went away without telling me anything, so Eleanor and I became friends." Half her mouth curled in a sheepish smile. "She's the only person who didn't think you were perfect and wouldn't scold me when I complained about you. But when she told me her plans to steal Lester, I felt guilty. I was angry, but I still loved you and didn't think you deserved that." She looked down at her hands now folded in her lap. "I got your letters, all of them, the next day, three days ago, and I felt even worse. Since I've been in the family way, I've been staying at my parents' so the letters had to go to Chicago before they got to me. My parents didn't want me to come; my mother said it was too dangerous. But I came anyway."

I tried to be happy for Jane, but jealousy still scratched at my insides. I stared at the other happily visiting patients while I collected my thoughts.

"I don't understand. Why would Eleanor do that?"

"It's because of that time when you were kids."

"What time?"

"You don't remember it at all?" Jane asked.

I shook my head. I combed through my mind trying to remember the moment Eleanor decided to hate me.

"She said she got her mother to come over. All you showed was a rock. She wanted her mother to look in your pockets, but she wouldn't do it."

Time seemed to stand still, and then it all came flooding back. "I think I remember," I said. I smiled as I remembered. "I wouldn't have been able to tell you why at the time, but now I know it was when I was falling in love with Lester, and I wanted to impress him. Hard work is what seemed to get his attention and admiration, so I did my best to always be doing something productive in case he saw me.

"One day, I walked by to see a cooker of clams all boiled and ready to be cleaned. So I drained them and started to separate the meat from the shells. I looked down and saw a pretty, smooth rock, so I picked it up and put it in my pocket. Just then, Eleanor ran up with her mother, yelling, 'She's got it. She took it. Ask her.'"

"What happened then?"

I crossed my legs and rested my chin on my palm, my elbow on my knee holding my head up. "I'm thinking." I switched my leg crossing and wrapped my arms around my middle. "Mrs. Lamphere asked me what I'd found. I wasn't sure what the fuss was, so I stuck my hands in my pockets and pulled out the rock." I turned to Jane. "I didn't think it was so bad. I have been talked to more harshly than that by my father hundreds of times. I remember Eleanor's mother said to her, 'Child, I don't have time for this nonsense. Get back to work.' Then she smiled at me meekly as if to apologize for the trouble. Eleanor stomped around, pushing the shells this way and that until she just walked away."

"Eleanor said she'd found a pearl that day. Or at least she thought she did. You remember how she never wanted to get her hands dirty?"

I did. I wondered if she'd changed. My willingness to get to work was something Lester said he'd loved about me. At one time, he wouldn't have looked twice at someone so prissy and stuck up. Maybe he'd changed his mind. There were plenty of hard-working men who wanted prim, proper, and smooth-skinned wives to meet them after a long days' work.

"Instead of reaching in herself," Jane said, "she went to get her mama. She saw you put something in your pocket, the rock, and assumed it was the pearl."

"But it was so long ago. We were girls. We were never friends, but I never had any arguments with her."

I stared at Jane's face. There was something she wasn't telling me. There had to be more. Jane looked at me out of the outside corner of her eye.

"It's Lester," she said.

"Lester?" That day I'd seen them talking at the blacksmith flooded back into my head and my heart pounded.

Jane turned toward me and grabbed my hands, an apologetic look on her face. "Eleanor said she had almost let the pearl incident go. She said everyone else loved you, and she never heard of you stealing anything else. Plus, you never got rich, so she thought maybe she was mistaken about seeing the pearl after all. Even so, what good is a pearl anyway if you hide it away? So she figured even if you still had it, you were not getting any more good out of it than she was.

"Eleanor said she'd had her eye on Lester for a while, but he never seemed to pay attention to her or anyone else. She got tired of waiting and asked him to go for a walk one Sunday." Jane laughed. "Can you imagine?"

"Did he go?"

"My guess was he was so shocked that all he could do was agree. But that was it. Eleanor said the very next Sunday, she saw you and Lester going off together."

"I remember that. I was so happy that Lester finally paid attention to me, but ..." My heart sunk and I swallowed. "But I guess he just did it to get away from Eleanor. Maybe he never really loved me anyway."

"Don't say that. That may have been the reason he asked you the first time, but it wasn't why he kept asking. Lester loves you. Whenever I've seen him and asked about you since you've been here, he gets the saddest look in his eyes. He misses you terribly."

"Then why didn't he just turn Eleanor away?"

"I don't know," Jane said. "Maybe he's just lonely. That's why you have to get out of here and get back to him. He can't bear to be without you, but he doesn't want to be alone. I think he's giving up hope that you'll get well."

I didn't tell Jane, but I feared that he'd given up hope on being a father, too, and perhaps he saw Eleanor as a solution.

"How am I going to do it, Jane?" I asked.

Visiting hours ended too soon, so Jane and I devised our plan with our code through seemingly innocuously written letters about the weather and progress of my treatment. I also sent letters in code for Sarah that Jane passed on to Sarah's cousin, Esmerelda. I hadn't heard from Lester in weeks, and figuring how busy he was with Eleanor, I didn't bother to try to write.

In whispers, as we waited in line for our cold weekly baths, I told Sarah the plan. "We're going to break out during visiting hours. Jane and Esmerelda will be hiding just outside the asylum boundary with horses. We'll walk that way, and when nobody is looking, we'll run through the bushes, get on the horses, and go as fast as we can."

"Do you think it'll work?"

The truth was I hoped so and it was the best plan we could devise, but I wasn't so sure. It seemed too simple, but I didn't want to worry Sarah.

"This place is like jail, but there are no bars once we get out of the building, so it has to be easier to escape from here than from jail." Sarah put her hand over her mouth to stifle a giggle. It was nice to see her smile.

"When?" Sarah whispered. It was my turn and I was dragged into the tub before I could answer that it would be quite a while. Jane had to deliver her baby first and then put everything in place.

*****

As warm as it had been for February, it was just as cold for April, like the conditions had flip-flopped. I sat in the cold parlor, watching the flurries, examining stray snowflakes as they landed on the window and eventually melted.

"Pearl Sinkey!" I was startled by the orderly and my heart began to race, wondering if my luck at avoiding the staff's wrath had finally run out again. I stood and walked toward the robust woman as slowly as I could.

"Well, hurry up. They ain't going to wait all day. Visitor!"

She thrust what I had since learned was one of the several better-appointed visiting dresses and sweaters into my chest. I had also learned that no privacy would be provided, so I changed as quickly as I could, folding my asylum issued dress neatly and setting it on a chair.

I still winced at her thumb and index finger pinching my elbows, not having enough visitors to get used to it, I suppose.

The joy that began to fill me at seeing Lester quickly faded. At Lester's side when he stood to greet me was Eleanor, dressed in her Sunday finery. Her coat's collar was lined with fur and her hat had so many feathers it looked like there was an entire bird up there.

"Is everything alright?" I asked. "Grandmother?"

"Everyone is doing fine, Pearl. Eleanor had mentioned that she would like to visit, so we decided to make the trip. It was nice and warm out when we started off, but it sure changed." He laughed and nodded at Eleanor.

I was in shock. It was like a dream. Like the dreams I occasionally had of Lester taking to drinking heavily but was so nonchalant, like it was an ordinary occurrence while I seethed. He didn't seem to have the slightest bit of qualm about bringing the woman who was trying to steal him away from me to where I was locked up in an insane asylum.

"Why don't we sit down?" He pulled chairs together in a triangle arrangement so we could all face each other. "Except for today, it has been such a lovely spring."

"Oh, yes, it has," Eleanor said. "My flowers are already starting to bloom." She smiled at me like we were old friends, which I guess we were in a way, but I knew better. Why didn't Lester?

"Planting started this week. And the clamming will soon be in full swing, though I suppose if this weather keeps up, they'll have to take a break. Wouldn't want to mess with old man river in this weather." He laughed and slapped his knee. Eleanor giggled and touched her lips with her fingertips. This had to be a dream; it was too much like a dime store novel not to be. He looked at my sober face and said, "'Course, you needn't worry. These spring cold spells never last long. Any snow that sticks will be melted in no time."

The next hour passed in much the same way. Lester and Eleanor chatting amicably and aimlessly about everything I was missing and me staring at them bewildered and befuddled.

Finally, Lester excused himself. When he was out of the room, Eleanor leaned toward me and whispered, "I had to see it for myself. But now I see you're as cuckoo as a clock. Lester deserves better, and I intend to be that better. I suggest you just let him go. He'll file for divorce and then we'll get married. He'll forget about you. If somehow you're able to convince them here to let you out, I'll make sure that it doesn't last long and you'll be back here before you can snap your fingers. I promise you that."

I couldn't hold it in any longer. I raised my right hand and slapped Eleanor square on her cheek. She fell back into her chair, a look of shock on her face. Before I could make another move, Lester was next to her and an attendant had my arms pinned to my sides.

"Pearl, how could you?" Lester asked. "We came all this way. And Eleanor, especially, your friend and mine. She's been such a help since you've been away, and she's constantly asking about you, so concerned she is."

He and Eleanor stared at me, but I didn't give them the apology for which they waited. I didn't struggle in the attendant's hold. In a rare act of kindness – it really was like a dream – the attendant let me go and said to Lester and Eleanor, "Sir, Madam, I think it's best that you leave now. Ms. Sinkey isn't feeling well."

The look on Lester's face haunted me for days. I couldn't believe he could be that naïve. He looked so hurt, confused, and completely beside himself as to what he should do with me. It was like this fear that I would never be normal again washed over him and spilled out through all of his pores. I wondered if he was right.

CHAPTER SIXTEEN

On Saturday, April 25, 1909, as the attendants were stuffing themselves again on pastries and the doctors were distracted by dancing with the patients, I motioned for Sarah to sit next to me. I smiled at her and whispered through my clenched teeth, "It's tomorrow."

She looked at me, squinting her eyes. "What's tomorrow?"

For fear of being overheard, I'd purposely avoided talking about our plan to escape with Sarah. The poor thing, she must've have given up hope on it like she had on everything else. "It's that day we talked about; the day the horses go free."

Her eyes lit up and she grinned. She leaned her ear toward my face.

"Two-ten in the afternoon," I whispered.

She nodded. "Same as we talked about?"

I nodded back. We tapped our toes to the music. I could feel the anticipation emanating off Sarah and hoped we were the only ones who could tell something was coming.

The next afternoon, as I waited for Sarah, Jane, and Esmerelda among the fledgling rose blooms, I thought back to the rare, warm late October days when I'd steal away to eat my dinner along the river, the sun sparkling on the rippling water. Sometimes, I was happy to sit and bake beneath the weakening sun, thinking perhaps I should find a shade tree to save my complexion, when a burst of cool wind would provide relief. On the dark days when things were particularly bad at home, I'd watch the water flow on its way, wishing there was a way to jump in and allow it to carry me away, if not in the depths, at least to the Gulf of Mexico, and something different to see.

Perhaps if I never had a child, that could be a way I could be content. Over the last weeks, I realized that if I continued to allow my body to shut itself off from Lester, I would be guaranteed to never have a child. If I could open myself up to him, I may or may not have a child one day, but I could still be a real wife and have a happy marriage if Eleanor hadn't already gotten him. I'd realized that was really what I needed all along. I did so love Lester. Though he was naïve when it came to romantic relationships, he'd always been so kind and under-standing. I might never have a child, but I at least had Lester, or I hoped I still did. I decided that being close and really married to Lester in all ways would be enough, and I would accept the fate of whether or not we would ever be blessed with any children. I hoped that Lester could do the same.

And I thought if I couldn't be a mother, at least seeing different things may provide a bit of similar joy. With motherhood, you saw something new every day because your child was continually changing, growing. Of course, I knew there would come a day when the child would be on its own, and then one could hope for grandchildren to spoil and watch grow.

I giggled out loud remembering something my grandmother had told me once in confidence a few weeks before Lester and I were married.

She said, "Children are wonderful, but you need to know that at times, they seem to grow so slowly, and the days become a monoto-nous tedium that you wonder if they'll ever be grown. And then, like that," she snapped her fingers, "they're gone. It was only when those days were over that they seemed to fly by."

How I missed my grandmother and hoped I'd get to hold her hand one last time.

The Catholic church's distant clock chimed two; Jane should be there any second. I knew that Sarah understood what time to be there. She wouldn't have forgotten; her freedom was too important to her. Something must have happened. I snuck back inside, peeking around corners and ducking back and flattening myself against the wall when I saw or heard someone approaching. All the patients on the second ward were sent outside for the warm afternoon and were not supposed to be inside.

I finally found Sarah strapped to a chair. It was made entirely of wood, it's back tall with curved sides sticking out from it. Buckled belts attached to the curved sides held her arms and another one strapped her feet together on the floor.

"Hurry!" She struggled against the straps holding her down. "They'll be right back."

I ran to her, unbuckling and untangling as fast as I could. She began to whimper as I struggled. "We're going to be too late. Jane and Esmerelda will already be here and they'll think we're not coming," she said.

"I know Jane; she'll wait." I looked up to see a panicked look on Sarah's face. "And she'll make Esmerelda wait, too. If only I could get this…" Finally, the last strap broke free. I grabbed Sarah's hand and pulled her from the chair. We ran, miraculously not running into any staff, though with the patients safely occupied outside, other than the few with observation duty, they were likely all gorging themselves on fruit and cakes. When we got outside, I yanked Sarah's hand to slow her down.

"We can't run," I whispered. We walked the path as close to our planned meeting spot as leisurely as we could. I hoped that the attendants weren't aware of where Sarah was supposed to be so wouldn't think anything of us walking together as we often did. When further proceeding along the path would take us away from the spot, I looked around until I was as sure as I could be nobody was watching, and then I leaped for the nearest bush, pulling Sarah with me.

As we waited, I felt the seam of the bloomers I'd fashioned from my bed sheet, stitched together with thread smuggled in by Jane during her last visit, hoping they would hold. I heard rustling in the next row of bushes. It was the sign. I walked to them slowly. I could see Jane through the leaves. Looking back to make sure the orderlies' attentions were still elsewhere, I stepped into them, the rough branches scratching my skin as I dropped my skirt and ran to Jane, Sarah close behind me. After a miss-step, I jumped on the horse behind her. Sarah did the same, jumping behind who I assumed was Esmerelda. I wrapped my arms around Jane's waist, closed my eyes, and braced myself not to fall off as she kicked the animal's sides and we took off. Last autumn's leaves crunched under the horse's hooves. It sounded like splitting wood and I was sure we would be found out. When I couldn't hold it any longer, I drew in a deep breath. I cracked open my right eye, sure I would find a stampede of orderlies chasing us, but no one was there. Jane slowed the horse to a trot.

She squeaked, "I can't breathe."

I loosened my grip.

"Is anyone after us?"

I twisted my head to look behind and all around us. "I don't think so."

"Esmerelda and Sarah?"

"They're still there, but back a ways."

The horse slowed more and stopped. "Why are we stopping?" I asked.

"The horse needs to rest. Just keep an eye out. We're far enough ahead now that we'll be able to hear anyone coming and can get going fast." She jumped off and started laughing.

"What's so funny?"

"It's just … you … up there … in those bloomers."

I looked down. The seam on my right leg had come loose, leaving the material from my knee to the ground flapping like chaps.

"I never was much of a seamstress," I said, relaxing into a laugh, realizing, I'm free.

Sarah and Esmerelda joined us within seconds. They jumped off their horse and hugged, exclaiming how happy they were to be seeing each other. When they broke apart, Sarah approached me. She grabbed me and hugged me tighter than I'd ever been hugged before.

"Thank you so much, Pearl." She let me go and looked at Jane. "You too, Jane. I don't know what I would've done without you. Probably rotted in that place."

"I'm just so glad it worked," I said.

"Esmerelda says that we need to part here. She's going to take me to Cedar Rapids to stay with her brother and sister-in-law. He's a lawyer and will keep me out of the asylum legally and help me get my son back."

I hadn't thought about anything that would happen after we'd left the asylum. I knew that Jane would convince Lester of my sanity and I would be safe since I'd been there voluntarily. But it was different, and much more dangerous, for Sarah who had been committed against her will.

"I'll miss you," I said, holding back tears.

"I'll miss you, too." Sarah hugged me again. She hugged Jane, too. "I'll write you. Pearl Sinkey of Camanche, Iowa. I'll send my address. Will you write me?"

"Of course I will. And when everything is all settled, maybe we can arrange a visit. I'd love to meet your son."

Sarah smiled. "We will definitely. We'll make sure."

I watched them as they rode away, sending all of my best wishes that everything would work out for Sarah and her son.

I was about to turn my attention back to Jane when I heard a creak behind us, like an old door. I jumped. "What was that?"

Jane looked up. "I think it's just the trees pushing against each other in the wind." She took an apple, canteen, and a shallow dish from a saddle bag. The horse chomped the apple down while Jane poured water into the pan. She held it up to its snout. The animal sniffed, looked around, and seeming to resign herself that it was the only option, she lapped up the water.

"Is it in here?" I asked, peering into the dark leather bag.

"Other side."

I unfastened the other saddle bag, reached in, and pulled out the skirt Jane had brought me to change into. I opened the waist and put my legs into the hole. I struggled to yank the tight waist over my hips. It wouldn't close so I left it undone. Another loud creak. Or was it a scream? I jumped again and goose pimples erupted on my arms.

As soon as the horse was rested, we continued. Jane had rented it from a livery two towns over. In an overabundance of caution, she didn't want to rent one from in town and raise suspicion. We got to the train station right at the last all aboard. We flopped in our seats, leaning on each other, trying to catch our breaths. We watched the world go by and dozed, trading places every now and then so we each had a turn at the window.

The train dropped us off in Davenport where we caught the interurban. My heart that had been pounding as if I had been running rather than the horse didn't slow, matching the clank of the train on the railroad tracks and then the steady sway of the interurban.

*****

I turned the knob on the front door, anticipating a surprised Lester that would quickly turn to joy and relief as I ran into his arms. Perhaps I would not even have to explain myself until after we'd conceived our child. But when the door opened, it was not Lester's face I saw. Eleanor stared at me over Lester's shoulder as she embraced him.

I didn't know what to say.

Eleanor, in a silky voice, said, "It's alright, Lester. I'll take care of you. We'll be happy. I'll give you all the children you want."

Lester pushed her away and held her shoulders with straight arms. "No." His voice shook, "That's not ... I'm sorry if I ... but..." and then he must've noticed Eleanor's attention was elsewhere. He turned his head to follow her eyes' path. When he saw me, he jumped. Eleanor pushed herself in front of him.

"Stay back. She's dangerous. Mad. She's escaped; she'll..."

Lester seemed to have forgotten she was there as he approached me, knocking her to the side. She stumbled.

"Pearl! You're here!" He wrapped his arms around me.

Eleanor, her face blazing with rage, said, "You ... we ... Lester and I ... I already gave him what you couldn't."

I pulled back from Lester's arms. "What is she talking about?"

"What?" He seemed to finally remember Eleanor was there.

"She said she and you..."

He swung around to face Eleanor. "What?"

Eleanor rushed toward him. "It's true. We're in love."

I'd never seen my Lester look so confused. "No, we're not." He searched my eyes. "I told her over and over that you were coming home soon. I told her that I would be loyal to you forever, even if you never came home. I was working extra to surprise you with new furniture. I made a new table and chairs and ..."

I stopped him with my lips on his. Of course, that was Lester. If there was a problem, he acted to solve it with productivity. And he was so honorable and kind, and he thought everyone else was the same, that he didn't discover Eleanor's manipulation. We held each other for several minutes, both having forgotten Eleanor was there, until we heard the door slam.

Lester and I held each other for what only seemed like seconds, but when we broke apart, the house was empty. I told Lester the truth. And then with Sarah's advice in mind, we were just patient and took our time. One day, I relaxed open like a cooked-out clam and never looked back. Our daughter was born nine months later.

Saturday, December 2, 1967

I will be 80 years old tomorrow. Our daughter is grown and on her own now with grandchildren of her own, my great-grandchildren.

A lot has changed in the world. We have electricity, full indoor plumbing, indoor commodes, radio, and television. Our country has been through two world wars. Lester's great-nephew was a POW in Korea in the early 1950s. Over my life, I've found it difficult to be truly happy. I have had moments of great joy and got a lot of what I wanted, but it never seemed to bring the satisfaction I thought it would. I'm kind of like that Scarlett O'Hara, except not nearly so strong or cunning, I'd read about in *Gone with the Wind* 30 years ago. I also got to see the picture show they made of that book. I've never been able to get that book out of my head. I heard they'd banned it from schools and libraries. Such a shame.

Sarah and I got together once. She was on a book tour in Davenport, so I took the interurban down to see her. We had lunch and she told me about how she was able to expose her husband and get her son back. Her book sold many copies, and she spent a number of years touring the country as an advocate for asylum commitment reform.

The treatment of the mentally ill has changed so much since those days, too.

One thing that hasn't changed is the Mississippi River. Well, that's not true, those locks and dams changed it enough and the mussels are gone (or almost), but I mean the way it looks when the sun shines on it, creating shadows that look like fingers coming from the east, and then later swinging to look like fingers going east. And the blackness. Of course, there are more lights along the shore nowadays, but the water itself still looks like the black of ink, and the moon still streaks across it. And the water, it still runs all the way to the Gulf of Mexico. Even if the mussels weren't gone, buttons are now made of plastic, so the shells aren't needed any longer anyway.

Over the years, after the big question of whether we would have children was settled, the idea of marriage changed for me. Before and early in our marriage, I was deathly afraid of it turning out like my mother's and father's. In those days, divorce was unheard of and I was so afraid of being stuck where I was unhappy like Mama. I didn't think I could bear it. As the years went by, divorce became almost common and I accepted it as an option, but never took it. I never wanted to. It was like as soon as I became unafraid of divorce, it ceased to have power over me. I knew every day I chose to stay with Lester, and some-how, that made me feel better. It's rather ironic. We spend so much time trying to push things away that we draw them to us. Sometimes, if we can embrace it, accept it, and even love it, it ceases to be a threat.

I never did tell my family what had happened with my great uncle, Mason. I never did stop wondering if something more had hap-pened. I never found out what, if anything, happened with Aunt Gertrude either. But it stopped mattering. I forgave Mason for whatever he did; whatever it was, it was the war that made him do it. If something happened to Aunt Gertrude, too, she had moved on to have a wonderful life, which I knew from the postcards depicting beautiful places she sent me periodically. I was always curious, but if she'd figured out how to live and be alright, I didn't want to bring it back to cause any heartache. If she could go on to be happy, I knew I could, too.

Lester was a good husband. Occasionally, I got lonely because he was so focused on work, but I accepted it and even took advantage when I needed extra chores done around the house. I had my Jeannie and she was all I needed. How can I fault a man for being a hard worker? I did my part with supper and housework and he was happy just to work. And when he had a bad day once in a while, he'd tackle the big jobs like window washing. Thanks to his worker mentality, we lived comfortably. We weren't wealthy, but there was enough that I never had to take in sewing or washing like some of the ladies whose husbands were less industrious, even through the lean depression years.

We continued our Saturday night whiskey sipping, straight up and neat. When Jeannie was little, Lester would read her a story, tuck her in, and crack open the bottle while I enjoyed a leisurely bath. After my bath, I'd join him for a few sips, then after we were sure Jeannie was down for the night, he'd love me sweetly and unselfishly. If I'd felt ignored or put behind for work during the week, on Saturday nights, I was sure of Lester's love for me. Even though he's been gone eight years now, I still have a nip or two of whiskey on Saturday nights.

AUTHOR'S NOTE

At the time, there were two state insane asylums near Camanche, Iowa, the Iowa Lunatic Asylum in Mt. Pleasant and the Iowa Hospital for the Insane in Independence. There is no evidence to suggest that these asylums suffered from any of the conditions described in the story or that any patients were mistreated in any way. The asylum portrayed in my story is strictly fictional, though many of the conditions and occurrences were based on three books: *Ten Days in a Madhouse* by Nellie Bly, *Marital Power Exemplified in Mrs. Packard's Trial, and Self-Defence from the Charge of Insanity* by Elizabeth Parsons Ware Packard, and *A Secret Institution: Memoirs from a Madhouse* by Clarissa Caldwell Lathrop.

SELECTED BIBLIOGRAPHY

Barron, Hal S. (1997). *Mixed Harvest. The Second Great Transformation in the Rural North, 1970-1930*. The University of North Carolina Press: Chapel Hill.

Bengston, M.L., Graham, R. & Halsrud, D., Editors. (1986). *Camanche, Iowa Charter City History Book*.

Bennett, Mary. (1990). *An Iowa Album. A Photographic History, 1860-1920*. University of Iowa Press: Iowa City.

Bennett, W. (2010). *The American Patriot's Almanac*. Thomas Nelson.

Berry, V. & Hecker, C. (1997). *Roots and Recipes: Six Generations of Heartland Cookery*. Pelican Publishing Company, Inc.: Gretna, Louisiana.

Bowbeer, A., Editor. (1976). *History of Clinton County Iowa*. Clinton County Historical Society: Clinton, Iowa.

Clinton County Historical Society. (2003). *Images of America: Clinton Iowa*. Arcadia Publishing: Chicago.

Clinton County Historical Society. (2004). *Images of America: Clinton Iowa*. Arcadia Publishing: Chicago.

Clinton Herald. (2004). *Clinton Once Upon a Time Sesquicentennial Edition from 1855-2005, Volume I*. Newspaper Holding, Inc.

Clinton Herald. (2005). *Clinton Once Upon a Time Sesquicentennial Edition from 1855-2005*, Volume II. Newspaper Holding, Inc.

Copeland, Jeffrey S. (2012). *Shell Games. The Life and Times of Pearl McGill, Industrial Spy and Pioneer Labor Activist*. Paragon House: St. Paul.

Erickson, M. & Long, K. (1983). *Clinton: A Pictorial History*. Quest Publishing: Rock Island, Illinois.

Maulsby, Darcy Dougherty. (2016). *A Culinary History of Iowa*. American Palate: Charleston.

McLean, Alice L. (2006). *Daily Life Through History. Cooking in America, 1840-1945*. Greenwood Press: Westport, CT.

Meyer, Carrie A. (2007). *Days on the Family Farm, From the Golden Age Through the Great Depression*. University of Minnesota Press: Minneapolis.

Morain, T., Nielson, L. & Schwieder, D. (2011). *Iowa Past to Present: The People and the Prairie, Revised Third Edition (Iowa and the Midwest Experience)*. University of Iowa Press: Iowa City.

Parrot, Michelle, Editor. (1990). *A History of Private Life from the Fires of the Revolution to the Great War*. Harvard University Press: Cambridge.

Rasenberger, Jim. (2011). *America 1908. The Dawn of Flight, The Race to the Pole, The Invention of the Model T, and the Making of a Modern Nation*. Scribner: New York.

Reader's Digest. (1992). *Everyday Life Through the Ages*. The Reader's Digest Association Limited: London.

Reiss, Benjamin. (2008). *Theaters of Madness. Insane Asylums & Nine-teenth-Century American Culture*. The University of Chicago Press: Chicago.

Sage, L. (1987). *A History of Iowa (Iowa Heritage Collection)*. Iowa State Press.

Schlereth, Thomas J. (1991). *Victorian America, Transformations of Everyday Life, 1876-1915*. HarperCollins: New York.

Sicius, Francis J., Editor. (2009). *The Greenwood Encyclopedia of Daily Life in America, Volume 3*. Greenwood Press: Westport, CT.

Yanni, Carla. (2007). *The Architecture of Madness. Insane Asylums in the United States*. University of Minnesota Press: Minneapolis.

Wolfe, P. (1911). *Wolfe's history of Clinton County, Iowa Volume 3*.

ABOUT THE AUTHOR

 Jodie Toohey is the author of four other novels – *Missing Emily: Croatian Life Letters, Melody Madson – May It Please the Court?, Taming the Twisted*, and *Taming the Twisted 2 Reconstructing Rain*; three poetry collections – *Crush and Other Love Poems for Girls, The Other Side of Crazy*, and *Versed in Nature: Hiking Northwest Illinois and East Iowa State Parks*; one non-fiction book – *Book Marketing Basics: The 5 Ps.*

When Jodie is not writing poetry or fiction, she is helping authors, soon-to-be-authors, and want-to-be authors from pre-idea to reader through her company, Wordsy Woman Author Services. She lives in Iowa with her family.

Learn more about Jodie's books, download bonuses, and sign up to receive updates at jodietoohey.com.
Learn more about her authors' services at wordsywomanforauthors.com.

If you enjoyed this book, please consider leaving a four- or five-star review on Amazon, Barnes & Noble, Goodreads, or elsewhere.
Thank you!